THE BRADLEY SERIES

TRENA'S RODEO RIVAL

by Bernard Palmer

Back to the Bible
Lincoln, Nebraska 68501

10,000 printed to date—1977
(5-5609—10M—37)
ISBN 0-8474-6257-9

Printed in the United States of America

Contents

Chapter 1

"Do You Really Want to Go?"

Eleven-year-old Trena Bradley stopped suddenly in the hallway at Collinsdale school and faced her best friend, Bev Grantham. Hurt gleamed in her soft blue eyes. Bev and Trena had been best friends since the Bradleys had moved from Detroit to the northwestern Nebraska town of Collinsdale.

Trena thought that she and her friend would go through school in Collinsdale together and then on to college or Bible school when they graduated. All of her plans for the future included Bev. It just couldn't be true that the Granthams might be leaving town, she told herself. It couldn't be. Bev wouldn't be going away.

But that was what her friend was saying. Mr. Grantham was being considered for the position of assistant foreman at the Bar T Ranch, and if he got the job, the family would be moving. Trena was crushed by the news and the excitement she read in Bev's face. She could hardly believe it, but Bev actually *wanted* to go!

"When will you know for sure?" she asked her friend.

Bev stepped to one side so the other students

in the corridor could pass on their way to their homerooms.

"Mr. Calero—he owns the ranch—came in to see Dad last night," Bev explained. "He said the assistant foreman at his ranch is quitting, and he is looking for a new man for the job. He's considering two or three others, but he happened to remember Dad. Dad used to work at the Bar T Ranch a long time ago—before he and Mom were married—and Mr. Calero would like to have him back."

Trena had heard of the Bar T. It was one of the largest and best-known ranches in the entire area, though she wasn't sure of exactly where it was. Mr. Calero had moved to Nebraska from New Mexico or Arizona and bought it a number of years ago.

"Dad is supposed to think over the job," Bev went on, "and Mr. Calero is going to check the qualifications of the other men who have applied for the job. The first of the week the ranch owner will come in to see Dad and . . ."

Bev let the sentence hang in the air unfinished, but Trena knew what she was about to say. Her lips trembled, and the color slipped from her cheeks, leaving them sallow and drawn.

"Do—do you really *want* to go out there?" she asked, not wanting to believe her.

"Oh, yes!" Bev replied. "It's beautiful out along the river, and Mr. Calero is so nice. Dad says there isn't anyone in the state who is better to the people who work for him than Mr. Calero. He's already told me that he's going to let me have a horse to ride whenever I want to, and he has rodeos and picnics and all sorts of things for the people who work on the ranch in the spring and summer when things aren't so busy for them. When

6

you see the Bar T Ranch, you'll fall in love with it the same as I have."

Trena's heart weighed heavily in her chest. She thought Bev liked being with her as well as she liked being with Bev.

"When will you move?" she asked woodenly.

"Dad doesn't even have the job yet. That's why I was so anxious to see you this morning. Would you pray that Mr. Calero will hire him?"

Trena didn't know what she said in reply. She didn't want to pray that Mr. Grantham would get the job, but she was afraid she had said she would pray that he would. At least that was the way Bev took it.

"How far away is this ranch?" Trena managed finally. "And where will you be going to school next year?"

Bev's eyes sparkled.

"I'm sorry; I thought I told you!" she said. "I'll be going to school right here in Collinsdale! Haven't you seen the sign marking the road to the Bar T Ranch as you drove along the highway? It's only about 10 or 12 miles from where you live."

Trena smiled her relief. "I thought you would be moving so far away you would be going to school in Scottsbluff or some other town. I didn't know the Bar T was so close."

"No way," her friend replied. "I'll be going to school and church right here in Collinsdale. That's what's so neat about it."

That information changed things completely as far as Trena was concerned. They chatted excitedly about the prospects of Bev and her family moving to the ranch. Bev said she was sure Mr. Calero would let her have Trena out to the ranch on

7

Saturdays to go horseback riding. There were lots of horses around the place, and he was sure to find one gentle enough for Trena to ride. And there were always people from town who were driving out to watch the rodeos. Bev was sure they would be able to get together as much as they did now.

At that moment Kathy Downing came rushing up to Bev. She had hurried in from outside, and her dark hair was tousled by the March wind.

"Oh, Bev!" she exclaimed, excitement in her voice. "I just heard the news! Isn't it great that you'll be living at the ranch?"

"Dad hasn't got the job yet," Bev said, repeating a remark she had just made to Trena.

"I know that, but I heard my mom talking to one of the other women at the ranch. She said Mr. Calero told Daddy that your father is the best one he's talked to so far. I'm so excited; I can hardly wait! There's never been another girl my age at the ranch. We can ride the school bus together and go horseback riding and study together and everything!"

Jealousy darkened Trena's features. Kathy kept on talking, the words tumbling over one another. She was thrilled about the thought of having Bev live at the ranch and wanted to talk about all the things they could do together. But Trena heard nothing else that she said.

For two years Trena and Bev had been very special friends—closer than sisters. They shared secrets with each other that they never even considered sharing with anyone else. They liked the same sports, the same studies at school and the same kind of music. They enjoyed being together whether they were doing anything special or not.

8

They often got together to study, to read adventure stories or to work on the Bible correspondence lessons their mothers ordered for them. Now Trena was beginning to wonder what would happen to their relationship.

There were certainly going to be changes; there would have to be. For one thing, they were going to find it a lot harder to get together. The Bradleys were in and out of Collinsdale a dozen times a week. Any time Trena and her friend felt like getting together, they could manage. But if the Granthams moved out to the ranch, it would take some doing. The Bradleys hardly ever went down the narrow, twisting trail that led to the ranch buildings. Hardly anyone took that road unless he was actually going out to the Bar T. It was the kind of road no one traveled unless he had to.

But that was not all that bothered Trena. If Mr. Grantham got the job, and it certainly looked as though he would, Kathy would be living next door to Bev. They were both in the same grade at school, and there were no other girls around at the ranch. It was only reasonable that they would be studying together, riding home together and doing almost everything else together. Before long, Kathy would be Bev's best friend.

Trena stared helplessly at them. Kathy and Bev would be together so much and doing so many things together that Bev wouldn't have time for her. That's what bothered her more than anything else.

"I've got to run," Kathy exclaimed suddenly, her laughter ringing through the hall. "I've got to get a book back to the library, or Miss Hopkins will skin me alive. Let's eat lunch together. OK?"

9

Bev nodded. She saw that something was bothering Trena, and she wanted to be with her, but Kathy had a way of pushing in and taking over.

When the other girl was gone, Bev noted the time and said that they should get to their homeroom before the final bell caught them and they had to go to the principal's office for an excuse.

"Mother says there isn't even one other Christian working on the ranch, as far as she knows," Bev continued as they walked toward their homeroom. "As nice as Kathy and her folks and Mr. Calero are, they don't know anything about Jesus Christ. Mom says she wonders if maybe that's the reason why we're being given the chance to go to the ranch and live. Maybe God wants us to reach some of those people for Christ." She took hold of Trena's hand impulsively. "You and I will have a lot of opportunities to share Christ with Kathy. Maybe she will be the first to become a believer in Jesus Christ."

"That would be nice," Trena acknowledged thoughtfully, "but I doubt that she would be interested." She didn't know why she said that; the words just popped out.

Bev looked at her questioningly.

"What makes you say that?" she asked.

"I don't know," Trena answered. "She just doesn't seem to be the type."

"Dad always says there isn't any certain type of person who is easy to reach for Christ. He says everyone is a sinner and needs salvation. If the Holy Spirit has worked in a person's heart before someone talks to him about Jesus Christ, there is a good chance he will be saved. So let's pray for her," Bev said. "Shall we?"

*   *   *

That noon Trena hurried out of her last class and headed down the corridor that led to the school cafeteria. She was going to wait for Bev as she usually did. Then she remembered that her friend probably wouldn't want to eat with her. She was going to be eating with Kathy Downing. Trena slowed her pace deliberately. Kathy hadn't asked her to eat with them; that meant she didn't want her along. Well, if that was the way it was, she reasoned, she wouldn't bother them. She would eat alone.

Trena hung back until most of the students had gone through the line, and when she got her food, she found a seat at a table as far from Kathy and Bev as possible. She ate alone, feeling very sorry for herself.

That afternoon when school was out, Bev was waiting for her at her locker. She wondered where Trena had been at noon.

"We waited and waited for you," she said, "but you didn't come."

Trena's lips trembled slightly. "You were with Kathy," she said. "You didn't want me along."

Bev acted as though she wanted to deny it but had trouble finding the words. Or perhaps Trena had voiced the truth. At any rate, Trena felt terribly hurt. They hadn't even moved out to the ranch yet, and Kathy was already monopolizing Bev's time and winning her over until she preferred her company to Trena's.

The students on the bus that afternoon were excited about the district basketball tournament that was to be held the following week. The girl

11

sitting with Trena could talk of little else. Collins-dale had a good team this year, she said, and everyone talked as though they had a good chance of getting to go to the state tournament at Lincoln.

"Dad said if we get to play in the state tournament, we all get to go and see the games—our whole family, I mean." She drew herself erect proudly. "My oldest brother is on the first team, you know."

Ordinarily, Trena would have been as excited about it as her friend, but on that particular afternoon she didn't much care whether or not the basketball team won the district tournament. It wouldn't do her any good, she was sure of that. She'd never get to go to it. She never got to do anything!

That night when Trena was in bed, she remembered promising her friend to pray that her dad would get the job as assistant foreman at the Bar T. She had fought against it during family devotions that evening. They might have noticed that something was wrong with her, but she had said nothing that would indicate what the problem was.

Trena didn't see how Bev could ask her to pray that her dad would get a job that would make it necessary for them to move. At first, Bev's moving to the ranch sounded exciting to Trena, but now that she'd thought about it, she really couldn't see why Bev, or anyone else, would want to live on a ranch.

But she had promised her friend that she would pray about it, so she had to do it. Reluctantly, she got out of bed and knelt on the cold floor. Tears

12

clung to her eyelashes as she began to pray. It wasn't very easy to pray for something she really didn't want to see happen.

Chapter 2

Lonely

Trena didn't even want to go to school the next morning. She wouldn't have, if there had been any way she could have got out of it. She certainly didn't feel like going. But she knew what her dad would say about that. If she didn't have a fever, a sore throat or a broken leg, she would go to school, and that was that. Missing classes was not viewed lightly in the Bradley family. And so, reluctantly, she got on the bus with Jon and Tim.

At least she had kept her promise to Bev about praying that her dad would get the new job at the Bar T Ranch, she reminded herself as the bus jounced over the rough road. If her friend asked about it, she could tell her that she had kept her promise. But her heart had not been in it. In fact, she was secretly hoping that her prayers would not be answered.

She knew what her dad would say about that too. He was always talking about being honest with God, with other people and with yourself. As she thought about it, Trena decided that she was being honest with God. She had told Him how she felt about praying about Mr. Grantham's job opportunity. And she thought she was being honest with herself. She found it hard to pray the way Bev had asked her to. That was because her friend meant so much to her.

But she wasn't being honest with Bev. Bev had asked her to pray, and she had said she would. But deep in her heart, Trena knew she could not intercede with God in the way she usually did when she prayed about something for Bev. She ought to ask her forgiveness, but she didn't see how she could do that. Bev didn't want to have much to do with her as it was. At least that was the way Trena read the developments of the past few days. If Bev found out about Trena's unwillingness to pray for her dad, she would write her off her list of friends.

For the first time since her family had moved to northwestern Nebraska, Trena was lonely. And there was so little she could do about it. She already knew the kids in her class. There were several besides Bev that she enjoyed being with, but only Bev was a close friend. Only Bev was close enough and trustworthy enough to share her deepest secrets. Now all of that was over. Trena was still troubled about the problem as the school bus slowed at the city limits. And she couldn't think of any way to solve it.

Usually, when the bus pulled into the parking lot behind the school building, Bev was waiting for her nearby. And if she wasn't around, Trena lingered inside the front door or near their lockers until her friend came so they could have a little time together. She didn't remember how they got started doing that. She couldn't recall that either of them suggested meeting in that way, but most of the time they did. They had so many things to

16

talk about. They just had to see each other for a few minutes in the morning, at noon in the lunchroom, and after school before the bus pulled out.

That morning, however, Trena did not wait for her friend. She got off the bus as soon as it stopped and hurried inside without looking around to see if Bev was there. She was sure her friend would not be waiting for her. Why should she be? Trena asked herself, still overwhelmed with self-pity. Bev and Kathy were friends now. They probably wouldn't care whether or not she ever came around.

Trying to mask her disappointment, Trena went to her locker and put her coat inside. She was approaching her homeroom when Bev and Kathy caught up with her.

"Oh, there you are," her friend said, hurrying up and grasping her by the arm. "We've been looking all over for you."

Trena's gaze sought hers. Bev needn't think she could make her believe that. "The bus just got in," she said coldly. "It was here at the usual time." They could have found her in the parking lot if they had really wanted to. But they were so wrapped up in each other that they didn't think about anything else.

Bev acted as though she had not even heard the unfriendliness in Trena's tone. "We were a little late this morning," she said.

"I didn't even ride the bus this morning," Kathy put in. "Mr. Calero was coming to town, so I caught a ride with him."

"And," Bev exclaimed, "we've got the most exciting news!"

Trena winced. That could mean only one thing.

"I suppose your dad got the job he wanted at the Bar T Ranch."

"Who told you?" Bev asked, disappointed. "I wanted to surprise you."

"That wasn't so hard to figure out," she retorted, still cold and unfriendly. She would have turned and gone into the classroom, but Bev still clung to her arm.

"Mr. Calero called Dad last night and asked him to wait at the house until he could get in from the ranch this morning to talk to him. Today he told him that he had gone over the qualifications of the other applicants and decided there was no use in waiting around any longer. He was going to give the job to Dad, if he wanted it. And the wages and—and everything are so much better than Dad had ever thought they could be."

"So," Kathy broke in, "Bev and her family are going to be moving out to the ranch the first of the month. Isn't that wonderful?"

Trena murmured something. She didn't know what she actually said to them after that or what they said to her in return. All she could remember for sure was telling Bev she was glad she was getting what she wanted and hoped she would be as happy on the ranch as she thought she would be. Then she pulled away from Bev and went to her desk. Her friend followed her and whispered that she would like to eat lunch with her. Trena was about to accept, but then she hesitated.

"Is Kathy going to eat with you too?" she asked.

Bev nodded. The look in her eyes let Trena know that she did not understand the question. "Does that make any difference?" she asked.

18

Trena almost cried.

"You'll have a lot of things to talk about," she said lamely. "You won't want to have me along."

"But we do!" Bev said earnestly. "I do!"

Trena was distant and aloof. "I'll see," she muttered. "I may have something else to do at noon. If I'm not there, don't wait for me."

Trena didn't eat with Bev and Kathy that noon. Why should she? she asked herself. Bev had another friend now. They were going to be neighbors on the ranch and would be together all the time. Having Bev move hurt enough, but being replaced as her friend was more than Trena could bear.

*   *   *

When her mother called her to supper that night, Trena didn't feel like eating. But she knew there would be a lot of questions if she didn't, and she didn't feel like making any detailed explanations right then. As it turned out, however, her family saw how unhappy she was.

"Who's the big boyfriend now?" her younger brother, Jon, demanded. "And what'd he do? Dump you for somebody else?"

Her gaze was withering. "For your information," she stated, "there isn't any boyfriend, so he couldn't have dumped me for somebody else."

"I can find out. I can ask around at school!"

"You do that!" Trena exploded. "Ask anybody!" She pushed her chair away from the table, leaped to her feet and fled from the room. Her bedroom door slammed behind her.

Jon glanced uneasily at his folks. This was the

19

kind of situation that could get him into trouble, he decided. He hadn't meant to do more than rib Trena a little—the way she teased him—but it hadn't worked out as he had planned. Maybe she did get dumped by someone he hadn't known anything about.

"I—I'm sorry," he said to no one in particular. "I sure didn't figure on making Trena blow her cool the way she did."

His dad leaned forward slightly. "You're apologizing to the wrong people, aren't you, Jon?" he asked quietly. "We aren't the ones you hurt. It was Trena. She's the person you should be talking to."

Jon hesitated. Usually he enjoyed teasing his older sister, but it did bother him to know he had upset her so much.

"Do you think I ought to go talk to her, Dad?" he asked.

"Not right now," Mrs. Bradley said. "Let me talk to her first."

When Mrs. Bradley knocked on the door, Trena was lying across the bed, sobbing uncontrollably. Right then she didn't want to talk to anyone and did not respond to the knock. When she heard her mother's voice, however, she asked her to come in. Her mother was the one person in the family who would understand.

Mrs. Bradley came into the bedroom and sat on the edge of the bed. She quietly put her arm on her daughter's twitching shoulder. When the sobbing finally stopped, she asked Trena if she would like to talk about her problem.

"There's no use talking about it," she blurted out. "There's nothing you can do."

"That may be right," Mrs. Bradley answered

20

honestly. "There are problems other people simply cannot help us with. But there are times when just talking can make a difference."

Trena supposed that was true. It certainly hadn't helped her much to keep everything bottled up inside. Slowly, she began to relate what had happened. She told her mother about Bev's moving out to the ranch and how Kathy was taking over Trena's friendship with her.

"I don't think you have anything to worry about," Mrs. Bradley answered. "I'm sure Bev isn't going to stop your friendship the way you think she is."

"But you—you just don't know. Already Kathy is with her every minute she can be, and I—I feel dumb tagging along."

"The two of you don't have to pair off. All three of you can be friends."

"But you don't know how possessive Kathy is," Trena answered. "She's always talking about the things she and Bev are going to do and how much fun they are going to have on the ranch and everything. They don't want me around."

Mrs. Bradley did not try to argue with her daughter. Instead, she suggested that they pray about it.

"God can work this out," she assured her.

Together they knelt and prayed.

Trena felt a little better the next day, but that lasted only until she saw Bev and Kathy together again. They were laughing and talking excitedly and didn't even stop when they saw her. At least that was the way it seemed to Trena. She was so miserable she didn't ever want to see anyone.

At noon, however, Bev surprised her by seeking

21

her out and insisting that the two of them eat together. Trena could not understand it.

"Kathy's not going to like it," she said acidly.

"What does Kathy have to do with you and me eating lunch together?"

"You're with her all the time."

Bev brushed Trena's words aside, and the two of them went into the lunchroom and ate at a little table in the corner. Bev wanted to know what was wrong and why Trena had been avoiding her.

"Even Kathy has noticed it," she said. "You never want to be with me anymore."

Trena protested that it wasn't true. Her feelings toward Bev had not changed, and she hadn't been avoiding her.

"Only it seems that every time I'm with you, Kathy's there. I—I—" Her lips were quivering. "I thought you didn't want me to be with you."

Bev grasped her arm impulsively. "Don't ever say anything like that again!"

Chapter 3

An Invitation to Ride

Trena felt a little better after talking with Bev about Kathy and about the move Bev's family was making to the Bar T Ranch. Or she felt better until she saw that things were the same between Kathy and Bev. Kathy was constantly with Bev. When Trena had lunch with her best friend, Kathy was along or soon found them in the lunchroom. When she did locate them, she barged in whether she had been asked or not. When Trena and Bev met near their lockers, Kathy was there, asking if she could go downtown with them. And she always monopolized the conversation when the three of them were together.

"When you're living at the ranch, Bev," she would say, deliberately ignoring Trena as though she weren't even there, "we're going to pick out a good horse for you. I've already talked to my dad about it. He says you can have your pick. You can even have the sister to the horse I ride, if you want her."

Trena's eyes narrowed. She shouldn't have said anything; Kathy wasn't even talking to her. But she couldn't help it. "How can your dad say that Bev

23

can have her pick of the horses to ride? Mr. Calero owns the ranch, doesn't he?"

Kathy's cheeks flushed as though she had been caught telling something that wasn't true. "My dad's the foreman," she explained defensively. "He takes care of things like that. Even if Mr. Calero were going to give Bev a horse to ride, he would come to Dad first."

Bev caught the fire in the voices of her friends and changed the subject quickly.

"I might have to pick an old plug," she said, "if I'm going to have a horse I can stay on. I don't ride very well."

"I can teach you," Kathy countered. "I'll tell Dad that you need a gentle horse at first. After you learn to ride well—which won't take very long because we'll ride a lot—you can pick the horse you want for your very own."

And so it went. Trena tried to ignore the attempts of the other girl to exclude her from the conversation. She tried to be nice to Kathy, but it wasn't easy. Kathy seemed determined to take her place as Bev's best friend. And the way it looked to Trena, she was going to succeed.

* * *

Moving time for the Grantham family came all too soon. Trena didn't mention it to anyone, but every time Kathy informed her they were one day closer to moving, a knife twisted in her heart. Bev said things weren't going to be any different between them, but Trena knew better. They were different already. The two of them were never alone anymore. Kathy was always tagging along.

24

And most of the time, she and Bev talked about things that didn't include Trena.

Trena was surprised and somewhat disturbed when her dad told the family at the supper table one evening that the men of the church were getting together to help the Granthams move the following Saturday.

"If we leave it all to Peter," he said, "it'll take a week, but if we help him, we can do it in a short day."

"Hey, that sounds great!" Jon broke in. "And the kids can go along and go horseback riding."

"It's supposed to be a work day," 13-year-old Tim said scornfully. "Who's going out to the Bar T to ride horseback?"

Jon grinned. "Me, for one. And I'll bet I could find a lot of other guys who're interested. Right, Dad?"

Dr. Bradley knew his youngest son was only kidding about going out to the ranch to ride and smiled at him.

"Of course Mr. Calero might have something to say about it if 20 or 30 kids descended on his ranch asking for horses to ride."

Jon managed to scowl convincingly. "That's the trouble," he said. "There's always someone around to spoil my best ideas."

The project to help the Granthams move started with the men of the congregation but soon included the women and children. Mrs. Bradley was the first to suggest that they could help.

"Susan Grantham will need some help too," she said. "There will be dishes and pictures and clothes to pack and unpack and cleaning to do. I think they need more help than the men can give."

25

She called a couple of the women of the church, and they made plans to help too. They decided to have a picnic lunch at noon, and after the work was done that night, they would have a time of fellowship, closing with a brief dedication of the Grantham's new home led by the pastor. Everyone was excited about it.

Trena was glad that the church was going to help Bev and her folks move and that Mrs. Bradley had a part in planning what the women would do. That would show Bev who her true friends were. Kathy could talk big about all the things she was going to do for Bev, like helping her choose a horse of her own to ride. But it was the Bradleys who really got things done. And she was pleased at the way Bev responded. She was beginning to see that Trena was her best friend after all.

"Kathy and her folks just can't understand why so many people would put themselves out to help us move," Bev said. "Even Mr. Calero asked Dad about it. He offered to let us use a couple of the ranch trucks and said he'd get some of the men to help. When Dad told him we didn't need any more help, he had a good chance to share Christ with him. Mr. Calero seemed really interested. He said that he didn't know people put their faith in Jesus Christ to work to help others the way the Bradleys and the rest of the congregation were doing."

Trena felt warm and good inside. She had no idea things would work out that way. "Maybe this will be the means God has of reaching Mr. Calero and his family for Christ."

"And Kathy and her family," Bev added. "I've been praying and praying for her."

26

At devotions the night before the people of the church were going to help the Grantham family move, Trena shared what Bev had said.

"That's good news," Dr. Bradley replied. "The fact that Christians love and want to help each other does impress others. There's one thing that we must remember though. We can sometimes get to thinking that helping other people is the main purpose of our faith. But that's not true. We must live lives that are separated from the world and witness to others of our faith."

*   *   *

Early Saturday morning it seemed that half the congregation showed up at the Grantham house. By ten o'clock a procession of pickups had left their place in town, piled high with furniture, appliances and clothing. The moving was almost completed by the middle of the afternoon. Mr. Calero sought out the pastor and Dr. Bradley.

"If this is the way you treat your members," he said, joking, "I've half a notion to join your church."

"We'd certainly like to have you and your family attend our services," the pastor told him.

Color crept into the ranch owner's cheeks. "I'm afraid I'll have to pass on that one. We've never been much on religion." With that, he turned and walked away.

*   *   *

In Sunday school the next day Bev invited Trena to come out to the ranch the following

Saturday to go horseback riding with her and Kathy.

"Mr. and Mrs. Calero stayed last night after everyone else left. He told me that I could have some of my friends out to ride or do whatever we wanted to at any time. I told him that you are my very best friend, and he said you are especially welcome. I was to tell you that."

Trena's eyes brightened. She was almost ashamed of herself for being so upset about Bev and her family moving to the ranch. Maybe it wasn't going to be so bad after all.

During the next few days Kathy was as possessive of Bev as ever, but Trena managed to overlook it. She was even able to remain calm when Kathy pretended to be the one who had arranged for her to come out to the ranch to visit Bev and go horseback riding.

"I talked with Dad about it," she told Trena when the two of them were alone. "He said that since you are a friend of Bev's, he guessed it would be all right."

The tone in Kathy's voice was disturbing to Trena. She made it sound as though it would probably be all right for Trena to come out to the ranch, as long as she didn't come too often.

"I thought Mr. Calero talked with Bev about it," Trena said. "She told me he had said I can come out any time I want to. He would like to have me come and visit her. She told him that I'm her best friend."

Kathy winced. "That was after I'd talked to Dad," she said lamely. "He must have mentioned it to Mr. Calero, or he wouldn't have known anything about it."

Trena was sure that was not true, but she did not challenge Kathy about it. It really didn't matter who was responsible for the invitation.

Although Trena had done little riding, she had always loved horses. She had two or three pictures of horses in her room and a whole shelf of books about horses and taking care of them. She still bought new ones every chance she had. However, she had never had an opportunity to do much riding. It seemed to her that Saturday would never come.

At breakfast that Saturday morning Jon teased her about letting him take her place. "You don't know anything about riding," he said. "You'll just fall off and break something."

"I think I'll be able to ride as well as you," she countered.

"You don't really believe that. Come on, Trena. I'll go riding for you, and when I get home, I'll tell you all about it. OK?!"

Trena simply frowned at him and went back to eating her cereal.

*   *   *

Trena found that riding was more fun than she had ever imagined it would be. Mr. Calero himself came out to the corral and picked out a horse for her, a gentle 12-year-old that his own daughter had used when she was learning to ride. After she'd had a little experience, she could pick out a horse with more life, he said.

Trena had a natural talent for riding. She swung herself up into the saddle with the ease of one who had been riding for years. Her mount

29

responded to her touch on the reins, and she rode off with Kathy and Bev at a brisk trot.

Mr. Calero turned to Mr. Grantham, who was standing close by. "That Bradley kid rides like a pro," he said. "Do you suppose she's pulling our leg when she says she's never ridden very much?"

Mr. Grantham shook his head. "Not Trena. If she told you she's never ridden much, she hasn't. She tells the truth."

Mr. Calero pushed his hat to the back of his head.

"I've seen a few natural riders in my time, and I suppose you have too. She's one of them."

Chapter 4

The Ranch Rodeo

Dr. Bradley had an unexpected visitor on Monday afternoon. He told the family about it that night at the supper table.

"Mr. Calero stopped in to see me today," he began slowly, glancing at Trena.

"What's the deal?" Jon broke in before anyone else could speak. "Did he come to tell you not to let Trena come out to the Bar T to go riding anymore? Hey, Trena! Maybe he figured you should ride a rocking chair instead of a horse!"

She made a face at him. Fortunately for her, neither of their parents saw it.

"No, it was nothing like that," Dr. Bradley continued. "He used Trena as his excuse for stopping, but I think he really wanted to talk to me about the people of the church taking time to help Peter Grantham and his family move."

He went on to say that the owner of the Bar T had trouble understanding why anyone would take the time to help a fellow church member. He was curious to find out what the people got out of it.

"He couldn't believe that we would help the Granthams because we love them and that we didn't expect to get anything out of it for ourselves."

Mr. Calero said that no one had ever done a favor for him who didn't expect to get something from him in return. That gave Dr. Bradley the opening he needed. He was able to spend about an hour sharing Christ with Mr. Calero. He didn't trust the Lord, but he was very interested.

"We'll have to pray for him and his family," Trena said when her dad had finished.

Mrs. Bradley nodded. "And for the Downing girl too," she added. "I was talking with Susan Grantham Sunday morning after church. She said that Bev is very concerned about Kathy. She doesn't know the Lord and doesn't act interested in hearing about Him."

Trena did not reply. Guilt swept over her. She had promised Bev she would pray for Kathy, but she hadn't been doing it.

After a time Dr. Bradley brought the conversation back to Mr. Calero's visit.

"I haven't told you everything Gerard Calero said," he went on. "First of all, he told me that he likes the way Trena rides."

"You've got to be kidding!" Jon exclaimed, horrified that anyone could think his sister had more ability than he had. "Trena doesn't know anything about riding horses."

"I know more about riding than you do," she countered.

"That's enough, you two." Dr. Bradley paused for a moment before going on. "Mr. Calero called you a 'natural rider,' Trena. He said you are one of those rare persons who seems to ride well from the

32

very first—someone who doesn't have to be taught much about sitting on a horse."

The statement brought a smile of pleasure to her lips.

"But that's not all." He went on to tell the family that the rancher had gone out to the barn after the girls had got back from their ride. Kathy and Bev were about to leave their horses after watering and feeding them, but not Trena. She got a currycomb and brush and rubbed down her horse before turning him out to pasture.

"Mr. Calero said that any girl who would do that really has to love horses. He said that he had already sent you an invitation through Bev to come out to the ranch and ride any time you want to, but he was afraid you might not take it seriously unless he stopped and said something to me about it. He said you are welcome to come out to the ranch any time you want to visit Bev and Kathy or even to go riding by yourself."

Her cheeks flushed happily. She did love horses, but she didn't think it showed that much. And she hadn't expected the rancher to say anything about it—or to even notice it.

"And he has given us all a special invitation out to the ranch next Saturday for the first ranch rodeo this spring."

The Bradleys had never been to a ranch rodeo, but they had heard a lot about them. Everyone in northwestern Nebraska knew about them. All during the week the people on the ranch worked hard, but sometimes on Saturday they got together to have fun. There was bronc riding, calf roping and barrel racing. Rodeo teams from various ranches sometimes got together to compete against

33

each other. Some of the sponsors bought special trophies for the winners in each event and the championship trophy for the team winner. The entire Bradley family was excited about being invited to see the rodeo, but Jon was especially enthusiastic.

"Know what I'm going to do?" he informed them. "I'm going to ride a calf."

"*You?* Ride a calf?" Tim exploded scornfully. "You've got to be out of your skull. You've never done any riding, unless it would be on that billy goat of yours."

"That's all you know about it. I don't go around bragging about how well I can ride, that's all."

"I'd like to see you ride a calf. I dare you to try it!"

"Who's going to try it?" Jon blustered. "Just wait. You think I can't do anything, but I'll show you. I'll have Mr. Calero pick out the meanest, ugliest calf he's got on the ranch, and I'll ride him to a standstill."

"They don't have calf riding for boys your age, do they?" Mrs. Bradley asked hopefully.

"Sure they do, Mom," he said. "It's the main event, the way I get it. They have all the other things first. Then they bring on the calves. And that's when I'm going to show that brother of mine he's not so smart."

Mrs. Bradley wasn't sure she wanted Jon to try riding a calf. She knew he had never done any riding and knew nothing about it, but she also knew what Tim's needling him might cause him to do.

34

"Tim," she said quietly, "please quit teasing Jon."

"You don't have to worry, Mom," Tim said, laughing. "They pick out such scrawny calves nobody could get hurt trying to ride one."

Jon could not stand by and have his older brother laugh at him any longer.

"That may be what they do for the guys your age," he said, "but anyone can ask for a big, mean calf, and that's what I'm going to do." He didn't really know anything about it, but that was the way he would run things if he owned a ranch and had a Saturday rodeo, so he was sure Mr. Calero would do it that way. He glared at his brother. "If you think you know so much, why don't you ride? I dare you!"

"Not me," Tim retorted. "I know better. You're the guy who's doing all the bragging about how well you can ride. You haven't heard me say a word."

"OK! OK! You just watch me tomorrow. I'll show you how well I can ride!"

* * *

The ranch rodeo wasn't scheduled to start until shortly after noon. But Mr. Calero had Bev's dad stop at the Bradleys' on the way home from town with a pickup load of supplies. He took Trena to the ranch so she could spend a few hours with the girls. When she got there, Kathy and Bev were down by the chutes where the rodeo was to be held. Kathy was excited about the girls' barrel race and could hardly talk about anything else.

"I wanted to ride in it last year," she said. "I

35

had about talked Dad and Mr. Calero into it, but my mom wouldn't let me. She thought I was too young. This year she's already agreed that I can, and I'm so excited I can hardly wait. We're having the first one today. There won't be very many girls racing though," she concluded, "so I shouldn't have much trouble winning." She was proud of her ability and let Bev and Trena know it. "There aren't many girls who can ride well enough to give the top girls around here any competition."

Trena saddled up her horse, and she and her two friends rode off together.

"I shouldn't be wasting time by riding like this today," Kathy told them. "I ought to be working out with my horse. He's not used to having crowds around. I've got to spend a lot of time with him, getting him trained and in better condition."

"If you want to go practice," Trena told her quickly, "it's all right with us." In fact, she would be glad if Kathy left.

Kathy's eyes narrowed. "I don't believe so. Maybe it would be better not to work out this morning so he'll be fresh for the race."

Trena knew why Kathy didn't want to leave them, and the reason was not her horse. She didn't like the idea of Bev and Trena being together without her. She ate dinner with the Granthams and stayed with Bev and Trena until time for the girls' barrel race.

"Keep your fingers crossed for me, Bev," she said, "to bring me good luck."

"We'll pray for you," Bev assured her. "That will really help."

Scorn flashed in Kathy's smile as she swaggered

off. Every movement revealed that she didn't put any confidence in prayer.

"I've been praying and praying for her, Trena," Bev said, "and I've done everything I can think of to get her to let me share Christ with her, but she's always just like that. Every time I say anything to her she gets that superior look on her face and says something smart or walks away. I don't know what I can do to get through to her."

Trena was disturbed by her own attitude. She was somewhat shocked to realize that she was almost glad Kathy didn't want to have anything to do with Jesus Christ. It haunted her. Again and again it came back to her when she was reading her Bible or praying or when she was alone in her room at night. Now, however, she pushed it aside—or tried to.

"I talked with Mom and Dad about it," Bev continued, "to see what they would suggest. They said it's so hard to get people to listen when they are determined not to that there isn't much anyone can do about it. They said we would just have to keep on loving her and praying for her."

Trena winced and was glad when the announcer signaled the start of the barrel race.

"What do they do?" she asked Bev, grateful for the opportunity to change the subject. "Do they all race at the same time?"

Her friend shook her head. In the barrel race, Bev said, the riders race against time. The rider starts at a line that serves as both the start and the finish of the race. It could compare to home plate on a baseball diamond. A large oil drum is placed at the approximate location of each of the other three bases. The object of the race is to ride out, circle each of the barrels and get back to the finish line in the shortest possible time. If a barrel is knocked down, the rider is disqualified. There are three races, or go rounds, as they are called in rodeo language. The rider with the best average time wins.

It was obvious that the girls were competing in their first race of the season. Even the announcer remarked about the slow times they were turning in. Kathy had the best time for a single go round but was disqualified for knocking over a barrel on her final ride. She came back to Trena and Bev filled with bitterness and excuses.

"It was that horse of mine," she complained. "If only I hadn't let you two talk me into riding with you this morning instead of having a final workout, I'd have been all right."

Trena was about to retort hotly that she and Bev had nothing to do with Kathy's going with them, but it was time for the boy's calf riding.

Tim turned to his younger brother.

"OK, Jon, now it's your turn to show us what a good rider you are."

The nine-year-old swallowed hard.

"I—I—"

Another boy about his age took up the conversation.

"You aren't scared, are you?"

"Me, scared? What makes you think that?"

The announcer again asked the boys who were going to ride calves to come down to the chutes. Jon wiped the sweat from his face with a trembling hand and started to slip away.

Chapter 5

Mr. Calero's Request

No one paid much attention to Jon as he got
down from his place on the corral fence and moved
away from the small crowd. A few steps away was
the Bradley station wagon, where he could crawl
into the backseat and lie down on the floor. He
didn't know what he was going to tell Tim when he
got home, but he would think of something. Anything—even his brother's teasing—would be better
than risking his neck on one of those ferocious
calves.

They might be little, but anybody taking one
look at them could tell they were mean. They had
that gleam in their eyes. They'd not only buck a
guy off, but they'd also probably walk all over
him. No sir, he wasn't going to take a chance on
getting his neck broken by one of those wild
calves, even if sneaking out would mean that Tim
would be on him about it for a few days.

Jon didn't know why he hadn't kept his big
mouth shut. Nobody made him volunteer to enter
the calf riding. He had been bragging about how
well he could ride, and the first thing he knew, he
was telling Mr. Downing, the ranch foreman who

39

was in charge of the rodeo, that he wanted to ride a calf. He must have had rocks in his head to do a stupid thing like that.

Then the announcer called his name.

"Jon Bradley is wanted at the calf chute." He paused and repeated the statement.

With his hand on the back door handle of the station wagon, Jon froze.

"Oh, brother!" he groaned aloud. "Now I'm in for it!"

His only hope was to get down into the backseat of the station wagon and hide before anyone saw him . . .

"I'll get him!" an all-too-familiar voice sang out. "Hang on a sec!"

Tim, his own brother, was coming after him! When Tim came to the hospital—or maybe to his funeral—after the calf riding, Jon hoped he'd realize that it was all his fault! Everything would have been OK if it hadn't been for that older brother of his.

He was still standing near the rear of the station wagon when Tim found him. "Hey, Jon!" he called loudly. "Your calf's coming up next! Hurry up, or you'll delay the calf riding."

He turned sheepishly. "That's OK," he mumbled. "I don't want to hold things up. I'll just skip it."

"Oh, no you won't. They've got your calf in the chute. You've got to ride him!"

"Who says so?"

As though to answer his question, the announcer called for him again. Tim grabbed his arm firmly. "You aren't going to skip out now. If you don't come and ride the calf, you'll be the laughingstock of the whole county!"

Jon groaned miserably. He just hoped those people realized what they were doing to him. When he was taken to the hospital with two broken legs, they'd be sorry. But they wouldn't be half as sorry as he would be.

Reluctantly, Jon allowed his older brother to guide him back through the crowd and over to the calf chute. For some reason, the animal in the chute looked four times as big and fierce as he had a few minutes before. Somebody must have got mixed up, Jon told himself. They'd run in a big, ferocious calf for him. But there was no backing out now—not in front of all those people. One of the ranch hands helped him straddle the calf and showed him how to hold the loose rope that was around the calf's shoulders.

"The next calf rider is Jon Bradley!" the announcer said.

The gate swung open, someone hit the calf on the rump with the flat of his hand, and it jumped out of the chute. Jon clamped his heels against the lean sides of the calf and gripped the rope until the knuckles on his hand turned white. He was sure with every lunge of the calf that he was going to be bucked off, but somehow he managed to stay on until the whistle blew. Even then he clung to his bucking mount for several seconds before realizing that the ride was over.

A brief cheer went up from the crowd as he freed his grip on the rope and jumped off. For a moment or two his heart pounded, and he had difficulty realizing that he had actually finished his ride. He had stayed with the calf the required eight seconds, which was more than some of the other guys did.

And he had ridden a tough calf too. It wasn't everybody who could stay on a bucking animal like that. He suddenly realized that he shouldn't have worried. Actually, he could ride pretty well. There was no doubt about it—he was one of the best riders his age in the rodeo. By the time he reached the fence where Tim was standing, he was swaggering proudly.

"Well," he boasted to his older brother, "how'd that ride grab you? Not bad, eh?"

"You had such a tame little calf, Cindy could have ridden him," Tim said.

"That's what you think." He crawled between the board rails and took his place on the fence beside him. He didn't care what Tim said, he'd done all right on that calf. Now that the ride was over, he couldn't figure out why he had been so scared to do it. For a guy who could ride as well as he could, it was nothing. He could have handled a calf that was a lot bigger and meaner than the one they had given him, and he'd drawn about the roughest one in the whole event. He had to admit it: He was pretty good as a rider. He could ride as well as anyone his age and a lot better than most of them.

*   *   *

After the rodeo Mr. Calero sought out Trena and asked her to try barrel racing. She really didn't want to, but he had been so nice to her, she couldn't turn him down.

42

"I'll have one of the men put the barrels back in place," the rancher said.

"But I've never done it," she protested.

"I know. Don't try to break any records. Just bring your horse out the way the girls in the race did this afternoon and circle the barrels."

Mr. Calero had a different horse for her to ride than the gentle gelding she had been using. Blaze was a small, wiry quarter horse mare with a broad, muscled chest and sturdy legs. The little mare had been used in barrel racing before and knew exactly what to do. She blasted across the starting line in response to Trena's command, sped to the first barrel, circled it and pounded across the hard-packed ground to the second. Trena pulled her in too close, and Blaze caught the barrel with a hind leg. It teetered precariously before toppling over. By that time she had circled the third barrel and was racing back to the finish line.

"Bravo!" Mr. Calero exclaimed. "That was great! If I didn't know you were telling me the truth, I'd have a hard time believing that you've never barrel raced before."

Trena dismounted, shaking with excitement.

"Actually," she said, "about all I did was hang on. The horse did the rest."

"The horse in an event like this has a lot to do with it, that's true," the rancher said, "but you had much more to do with it than you think." He took the reins of the little mare. "Your folks are waiting. I'll take care of Blaze for you. You're coming out to ride next Saturday, aren't you?"

Trena hesitated. She didn't know whether she would be coming or not. Bev hadn't said anything about it.

"I want you to," he said. "OK? There are some things I want to talk to you about, and there's not time for it now."

She thanked him and started across the yard toward the station wagon. Kathy Downing caught up with her.

"What was that all about?" she demanded.

At first Trena wasn't sure what she was talking about.

"Why did you talk Mr. Calero into letting you try barrel racing just now? For your information, you were lousy. There's no use in your trying. You'll never get anyplace with it."

"But I didn't talk him into letting me try," she protested. "He asked me."

Kathy laughed scornfully. "You might make Bev believe that. You've got her fooled so much she'll believe anything you tell her, but I know Mr. Calero too well to buy that. He'd never ask anybody to ride in a race or take part in any other event."

Trena stared after her as she went storming across the yard toward her parents' house.

Bev was waiting for her at the station wagon. She was also eager to find out why Mr. Calero had asked her to ride for him. Trena told her all that she knew, which wasn't very much.

"I suppose Kathy asked about it too," her friend said uneasily.

Trena nodded.

"She wanted to know why I was trying to get Mr. Calero to let me race. She said I'm lousy and shouldn't even try." Her voice grew serious. "But Bev, I didn't push myself onto Mr. Calero. He came out and talked to me."

44

She didn't know why she was so defensive with Bev, but she felt as though she had to make her friend understand that she hadn't started the idea.

"I know." Bev nodded understandingly. She was well acquainted with her new friend. "She doesn't think anyone else can ride as well as she can in the barrel race. When I first came, she informed me that I wouldn't be able to ride well enough to make it worth my time—which is probably true." Bev paused momentarily. "But I'm so sorry this had to come up today. She finally promised she would go to Sunday school and church with me tomorrow. Now I'm afraid she'll change her mind."

"We'll all be praying that she won't change her mind and will go with you," Mrs. Bradley assured her.

Bev Grantham thanked her.

*　　　*　　　*

At devotions that night Mr. Bradley brought up the problem for discussion. He related the incident briefly and asked the family what Trena should do.

"Tell her to mind her own business," Jon said scornfully. "Kathy Downing doesn't own that ranch. If Mr. Calero wants Trena to learn how to barrel race, she ought to do it without paying any attention to Kathy or Bev or anyone else."

Tim and Mrs. Bardley weren't quite so hard on Kathy. They could understand how she felt, they said. She had been the only girl her age at the ranch for a long time, so she had had things her own way. Now Bev and Trena were around, and it looked as though Trena might cut in on her barrel racing. That was enough to make her jealous.

"You've got to face it," Tim said frankly. "Trena is going to be a great rider. Kathy probably is afraid she'll never have a chance to win if Trena is in the race."

"Doing what Jon suggested is the easy way," Mrs. Bradley said, "but we've got to think about Trena's Christian testimony and the fact that she and Bev are praying that Kathy will become a Christian too."

Trena flinched at her mother's remark.

"Are you trying to say that I ought to quit going out to the ranch to ride so we will have a better chance of sharing Christ with Kathy?"

Mrs. Bradley assured her that she wasn't trying to get Trena to give up riding at the Bar T Ranch. But Trena should be very careful not to antagonize Kathy and should do everything she could to be friendly to her.

"If I were you, I would pray about learning to barrel race," her dad said. "I think the Christian way would be to tell God that if this will be a stumbling block that might keep Kathy from trusting Him as Saviour, you want Him to show you or to remove the opportunity for you to learn. I think you ought to be willing to give it up if God leads you to."

Chapter 6

Jon's Big Plans

When she went to her room that night, Trena was deeply troubled. The warm glow she felt when Mr. Calero hinted that she should learn to barrel race was replaced with a dull ache, like a throbbing tooth that couldn't be filled or pulled. Her dad's remark about being willing to give up her chance to learn didn't seem fair, even if it might help her and Bev to reach Kathy for Christ.

After all, Trena hadn't asked Mr. Calero if she could learn to race. She hadn't even considered it until he came to her. And she still didn't know for sure what he had in mind; she was only guessing.

She knew she should put God's will first in her life. But what if He wanted her to give up learning to barrel race? Or what if He wanted her to give up going out to the ranch at all? Shouldn't she be willing to do it? Trena prayed about it for a long time, asking God to lead her, but it seemed that her prayers bounced off the ceiling like a ball.

She didn't like to admit it, but she knew what was wrong. What kind of an answer did she expect from God? She already knew that she should be willing to obey His will completely. But she was afraid He might lead her in a way she didn't want to go. And so she wrestled with the problem, trying to allow God to take complete control of the situation.

*   *   *

Kathy did not go to Sunday school or church the next day. When Bev went over to see if she was ready, she was still in bed and protested that she didn't have time to get ready.

"We can wait for you," Bev told her. "It's not that late."

"I'd never be ready on time. Besides, you won't want me around. You'll be with Trena, and she's a pain."

"Please don't say that," Bev protested.

"Why not? She doesn't like me, and I don't think she likes you much either. Not really. She only comes out here because she can ride when she comes to see us. She doesn't care anything about us. She's only using us so she's got an excuse to learn how to barrel race."

Bev tried to make Kathy understand that Trena had said nothing to Mr. Calero about learning to barrel race. He had come to her.

Kathy broke in rudely: "I already know that story, but I don't believe it. He's never asked anyone else to do that. And if you don't believe me, you can ask my dad. Why should he start that now?"

Bev had no answer for her question.

"Trena's just trying to make you believe something that isn't true." She drew in a deep breath.

"If she's an example of being a Christian, I sure don't want any of it." Her lips were trembling with anger.

Kathy wasn't being fair with Trena, Bev told herself. But there was no use in trying to reason with her. She had made up her mind that she was right, and there was no changing her. Bev was so disturbed she thought she would cry. It seemed to her that she had been praying for Kathy as long as she could remember. She had tried sharing Christ with her every chance she got. When that hadn't been effective, she had tried asking her to go to Sunday school and church with her.

Finally, Kathy had promised that she would go to the Sunday morning services with Bev. But now she was backing out because of this trouble between her and Trena. And by the way she sounded, it wouldn't do any good to ask her again. She had decided that being a Christian was not for her.

Bev left the Downing house and walked slowly across the yard to the place where she and her folks lived. She thought about telling Trena what Kathy said about her but decided not to. Trena had never said so, but Bev had the feeling her friend did not like Kathy very well. Something like this certainly wouldn't help. Instead, she told Trena that Kathy had decided not to come to Sunday school that morning, and again she asked her to pray for Kathy.

*   *   *

Jon's attitude toward calf riding changed dramatically in the week following his successful ride at the ranch. Two or three times he asked

49

Trena if she knew when the next rodeo was going to be held. Before she could answer, Tim broke in. "What's it to you?" he asked scornfully. "You haven't been invited out to see it."

Jon replied proudly, "Their top performers are invited to compete. They aren't asked to come out and watch what's going on."

"Top performers! Huh!" Tim exploded. "Riding a 100-pound calf doesn't make you a rodeo champion in my book."

"A 100-pound calf? Did you take a look at that big bruiser I got?" He took another piece of meat and started making himself another sandwich. "I just happened to get the biggest, meanest, orneriest calf in the whole event. Didn't I, Dad?"

Dr. Bradley was listening with obvious amusement. "Well," he said, "I don't know whether or not I would go quite so far as to say that."

"I would. He was a bad one! If he'd thrown me, he'd probably have turned and gored me before anybody could have got him away from me."

"Gored you?" Tim snickered. "With what? He didn't have any horns."

"You can talk," Jon went on. "But just wait until the next rodeo. I'll show you a ride you'll never forget." He finished making the sandwich and started to eat. "I've been doing a lot of thinking since my great ride last Saturday," he continued. "Being a natural rider must run in the family. That's got to be the reason I did so well in calf riding."

"Oh, brother!" Tim groaned. "Here we go again! Just because you were too scared of that

50

calf to fall off, you don't need to think that you're another Casey Tibbs."

Jon's eyes narrowed thoughtfully.

"I'm going to pretend I didn't even hear that crack," he said. "But who's Casey Tibbs?"

"I thought all of you great rodeo performers knew about Casey Tibbs. He used to be the world's champion saddle bronc rider. I figured you were planning to build a better record than he did."

The younger boy's frown deepened. He knew Tim was teasing him, and he couldn't let him get away with it.

"I don't know whether I'll be able to outride this Casey Tibbs or not," he said. "I haven't tried saddle broncs yet."

"And you'd better not try them," Mrs. Bradley broke in sternly, "if you know what's good for you."

No one said anything for a minute or two. Then Jon spoke, changing the subject. "I've been doing a lot of thinking about what I'm going to be when I grow up, Dad."

Dr. Bradley sipped his tea and returned the cup to the table. "You have?"

"I won't need a college degree on the rodeo circuit. I'll go out to the Bar T when I get out of high school and work for Mr. Calero during the winter. In the summer I'll ride in all the rodeos. I'll start with the little ones, and in a couple of years I'll be in all the big ones, like Denver and Cheyenne and Calgary."

Cindy gasped. "You can't do that, Jon! You might get hurt!" She turned anxiously to her mother. "You aren't going to let him, are you, Mother?"

"It will be quite awhile before Jon is old enough to do that," she said.

"I know," he countered defensively. "But a guy has to make his plans early. I figure I'll start out by riding in all the kids' calf riding contests I can find around here, just for practice. It's too bad they don't have prize money for the winners. I could make enough to buy my clothes and put a little in the bank."

*　　　*　　　*

There was no rodeo at the Bar T the next Saturday, but Mr. Calero had Kathy and Bev tell Trena that he expected her to be at the ranch early Saturday morning.

"But why?" Trena asked.

Kathy shook her head. She couldn't understand what it was all about, but she had the disturbing feeling that it had something to do with her favorite rodeo event—the only one she could compete in.

"He had you ride for him last Saturday," Bev said, hoping Kathy did not miss the significance of her remark. "Maybe he wants to tell you why."

Trena didn't know why he would want her to come to the Bar T, but the thought excited her. In fact, she could hardly wait until Saturday morning so she could talk to him.

When she got there, she told herself, Kathy would find out that she hadn't pushed herself onto Mr. Calero, if she didn't know already. She was glad of that.

She couldn't figure out why Kathy acted the way she did toward her anyway. If anyone had a reason to be upset, she did. Kathy had been trying in every way she could to break up her friendship with Bev. Whenever the three of them were together, she dominated the conversation constantly, talking about things that Trena didn't know anything about. And she was always making plans that included only Bev and herself.

When Trena got out to the ranch on Saturday morning, she expected Kathy to be there. She always had been around during her other visits. But this time she had gone to town with her folks. She told Bev that no one would miss her at the ranch while Trena was there.

"I don't know why she feels the way she does toward you," Bev said sorrowfully. "Nothing I can tell her will make her believe that you like her."

Mr. Calero came up just then, and Trena found out what he had wanted to talk with her about. He wanted her to take part in the girls' barrel race!

"I wanted Kathy to help you practice today," he said. "That's why I asked you to come out this morning. But she decided to go to town with her folks. So I'll have to help you get started and let you practice on your own."

Trena was so excited and frightened at the same time that she had difficulty mounting Blaze and getting her behind the starting line. She hadn't realized how excited she was about racing with the girls until now.

Chapter 7

Trena Learns to Race

Mr. Calero had a few instructions for Trena and even got on a horse and rode through the course himself to show her how to cut down her time and how to cut close to the barrels without knocking them over. After going over the course two or three times, he had Trena try it while he stood on the corral fence where he could see exactly what she was doing.

"That's it! That's it!" he shouted in encouragement. "You're doing great!"

He jumped off the fence when she had completed the course and took hold of the reins while he talked to her.

"You're not going to have any trouble picking up the tricks of barrel racing, Trena. With a little practice you'll be able to compete with the rest of them. You're going to be a good addition to our rodeo team when we start competing with some of the other ranches."

Trena was not so sure. "I don't feel that I'm doing it right, Mr. Calero," she said, "but I don't know enough about it to know what I'm doing wrong."

He scratched the horse's nose affectionately.

"You're doing fine," he assured her, "but you do have some things to learn. You've got to get your horse running at top speed from the instant you leave the starting line, and you've got to hold her closer to the barrels on the turns. But don't worry about those things. They'll come to you easily as you practice."

He turned to Bev. "And now, Young Lady, I've got to talk to you. Why aren't you entering the barrel racing? Don't you know we've got to have all the good riders we can get on our rodeo team when we start competition?"

Her cheeks flushed. "To be truthful with you, I didn't figure I could ride well enough for that."

"You can't give up so easily." His face was so serious she didn't know whether he was joking or not. "We've got the reputation of the ranch to think about. Your father's the assistant foreman here. If you don't take part in at least one of the rodeo events, you'll make the Bar T the laughing-stock of the whole area. I won't even be able to go to town. All my friends will ask me what kind of an assistant foreman I hired if his daughter won't have anything to do with rodeos. What will it be?" he demanded. "Barrel racing or ladies' bareback bronc riding?"

Her eyes widened. "You've got to be kidding!"

"And what makes you think that? You can take your pick. Which one is it going to be?"

She nodded in the direction of the barrels.

"I rather thought that's what you'd decide on. Have your dad pick out a horse for you, and get with it. You and Trena can practice together." As

56

he turned, she thought she saw a twinkle in his eyes.

"Do you suppose he was teasing me?" she asked when she and Trena were alone. "He wouldn't expect me to enter the bareback bronc riding—would he?"

Trena laughed, swinging down from her horse to stand beside her friend.

"At the ranch rodeo I saw, they didn't even have a ladies' bareback bronc riding contest."

Bev nodded thoughtfully and grinned.

"That's right, isn't it? I guess he must have been joking after all. But I don't mind telling you, he had me worried about it."

"Isn't he nice?" Trena murmured. "I don't think I've ever known anyone so thoughtful."

"Like Dad says, he's the greatest. There's only one thing wrong. He's not a Christian."

Trena thought about that. It seemed strange to her that a person like Mr. Calero, who was so nice and considerate to everyone, was not a believer.

"Are you sure?" she asked.

"He says he doesn't need to be saved. He's going to live a life good enough that God will let him into heaven anyway."

"But it doesn't work like that. The Bible says that everyone has sinned and fallen short of God's standard."

"I know," Bev answered. "That's why we pray for him every day during family devotions."

"I've been praying for him, too, whenever I think about it; but I'm going to pray for him every day from now on. And I'm going to ask our whole family to pray for him too."

Bev's dad helped her pick out a horse that

57

would be good for barrel racing and gentle enough that she could have confidence in riding him. Then she and Trena practiced together. Bev enjoyed it much more than she thought she would before she tried it, but it was quite apparent that she was not going to be as skilled as Trena. Her friend seemed to know instinctively what to do. They both knocked down their share of barrels and thought they would never learn to ride well enough to compete in even one go round without disqualifying themselves. But Trena was cutting closer on the corners and breaking faster as she urged her mount to the next barrel.

They were still practicing when Kathy came home from town. She seemed surprised that Bev was riding too. That didn't bother her though. She acted glad to see her getting ready to compete in barrel racing, in spite of what she had told Bev earlier.

"I didn't know you were interested in it too, Bev," she said. "You and I can practice for awhile every night after school. I'll help you all I can, if you want me to." She glanced significantly at Trena. "It isn't as hard as some people let on. All you have to do is work at it."

Trena turned quickly away, her cheeks flushing. Why did Kathy have to be so disagreeable? Why did she have to keep needling her and trying to come between her and Bev? Trena had good reason not to like Kathy.

When Dr. Bradley came out to the ranch to get her that evening, Mr. Calero went over to the car and talked to him briefly. He wanted to ask if Trena could come out to the ranch a couple of afternoons a week after school to practice barrel racing. Someone from the ranch was always going to town, he said, so he could make arrangements to get her back and forth.

"I don't know why I'm so interested in seeing her learn to ride as well as she can," he said, "but she's got so much natural ability, I'm anxious to see what she can do with a little practice."

That was fine, Dr. Bradley told him, as long as the practice didn't interfere with her school work. Her grades had to come first; and if they started to slip, the trips to the ranch during the week would have to stop. Mr. Calero said he could understand that. He would feel the same way if Trena were his daughter.

"By the way, Gerard," Dr. Bradley said, "we're having a men's fellowship dinner at the church next Tuesday night. I'd like to have you be my guest."

Mr. Calero eyed him quizzically. "I'll have to see about that."

Dr. Bradley was disappointed, but he didn't show it.

"I'll give you a ring on Monday afternoon to see if you can work it in."

Trena was thrilled that Mr. Calero had made arrangements for her to be out at the ranch a couple of times a week in addition to Saturdays. Bev worked out with her too. Kathy Downing was around, but it wasn't the same. She already knew how to handle herself and her horse on the barrel race course. She practiced, but it really didn't make her any closer to Bev. In fact, it worked just the opposite. Bev and Trena were both learning. They were facing the same difficulties and problems. It was only natural that they would be drawn together. Trena didn't notice it at first, but Kathy was being left out. She often stood in a corner of the corral some distance from them, feeling sorry for herself.

Trena sympathized with her but decided that it served her right. If she hadn't been so disagreeable and determined to ruin the friendship between Trena and Bev, she would be included now and wouldn't be left alone so much.

*　　*　　*

The Bradley family prayed for both Mr. Calero and Kathy Downing regularly. Every night at devotions one member of the family would ask God to bring them to a saving knowledge of Himself. A couple of weeks after Trena started going out to the ranch to practice for the barrel race, Dr. Bradley asked her if either she or Bev were having any success in talking to Kathy about Jesus Christ.

"She's come to Sunday school once or twice," she said, "but we haven't had a chance to talk seriously to her. Whenever we try, she turns us off."

"I've seen Kathy a few times lately," Mrs. Bradley said, "and I can't help feeling sorry for her. She seems to be so lonely. Do you and Bev try to include her in what you are doing, Trena?"

She hadn't expected her mother to say anything like that.

"She won't let us," she said defensively. "We try, but unless she can run things, she doesn't want to have anything to do with us."

"I've noticed the same thing that your mother

has," Dr. Bradley put in. "Kathy does act as though she doesn't have a friend in the world."

"It's not our fault," Trena said. "We'd let her run around with us all the time if she would, but she's so disagreeable and unfriendly, nobody can stand her."

Dr. Bradley picked up his Bible.

"I think we ought to pray for you and Bev, Trena," he said quietly. "I know you've got a bad situation, but we should ask God to help you be kind and considerate and friendly to Kathy. You know, it's almost impossible for a Christian to share Christ successfully with an unbeliever unless he's a friend of the one he's trying to reach."

Trena was disturbed by the tone of his voice. It seemed to her that he was accusing them of causing Kathy to be unfriendly. The trouble was, she told herself defensively, her dad didn't know what Kathy was really like. He'd never seen how disagreeable and disgusting she could be. If he had, he wouldn't talk like that.

When their devotions were finished, Jon asked Trena about the next ranch rodeo. She thought it was to be held the following Saturday afternoon, but she wasn't sure. Mr. Calero had said something about it the last time they practiced.

"You can find out for sure, can't you?" Jon asked.

She supposed she could, she told him. In fact, she would have to find out if she was going to compete in the girls' barrel race.

"I can't figure it out," Tim said. "I was sure Mr. Calero would check with you, Jon, to see if you would be available before he scheduled the rodeo. It would be a terrible failure if you weren't there to please the crowd with your great, death-defying riding."

Jon scowled at him. "You're just talking that way because you're jealous. I've been trying to decide whether I ought to ask Mr. Calero for a bigger calf this time. I've got to have a challenge, or it won't do any good for me to ride."

Chapter 8

Jon Rides Again

Trena was right about the ranch rodeo's being held the following Saturday afternoon. She had asked Bev, who wasn't sure, but the next time they were at the Bar T, Mr. Calero told them to be ready to ride in the barrel race. He had already put their names on the list of contestants.

"That goes for both of you, Bev," he said, frowning seriously. "Just remember, if you don't want everyone to laugh at the Bar T, you'd better win. Understand?"

She tried to tell him that she was far from being ready to ride in competition, but he would not even listen to her. She had been practicing for almost three weeks, he said. That ought to be plenty of time for anybody to learn everything there was to know about barrel racing.

That wasn't true, of course. Barrel racing was an exacting event that took skill and constant practice. But his eyes twinkled as he spoke. He was only trying to give Bev enough confidence in herself that she would do her best on Saturday afternoon.

Jon, on the other hand, had plenty of self-confidence. He didn't mind letting everybody know that he was ready for the calf riding event and was concerned only about getting a calf that was tough enough to test his riding ability.

"I've been wondering if I ought to ask Mr. Calero to pick out a special calf for me—one that's bigger and meaner and tougher to ride." He glanced at Tim to see if he had succeeded in irritating him. "After all, I don't want to disappoint my fans. We performers have our audience to think about."

He succeeded in getting a response from his older brother: "I just wish you would get a big calf," Tim told him. "He wouldn't have to be any tougher than the one you rode the last time—just a little bigger. You'd find out soon enough what a good rider you are."

Jon grinned. "I think the newspaper is going to send their photographer out to take pictures of me," he said. "And I know the radio and TV stations at Scottsbluff would have a reporter and cameraman at the rodeo if they knew for sure that I was going to ride."

Tim suddenly had a terrible thought. "You didn't go to the newspaper office and tell them you're going to ride at the Bar T rodeo Saturday, did you?"

"They like to have tips about important events," Jon hedged. "After all, I have my fans to think about. You wouldn't want me to disappoint half the county, would you? Let's put it this way: If Casey Tibbs were riding at the Bar T today, don't you think people would want to know how well he did?"

Tim shook his head disgustedly. He had never

known anyone so conceited. "I don't even want anyone to find out that you're any relation to me." He turned to Dr. Bradley. "If Jon did that, none of us will ever be able to live it down. I think I'll change my name and go up into the mountains and find an old cabin so far away from any town that no one would possibly have heard of Jon Bradley."

Jon was delighted with the reaction he was getting from Tim—it couldn't be any better. "Don't forget about radio and TV newscasts," he reminded his brother. "You won't get away from the big name I'll be making for myself. You might as well get used to the idea that you have a celebrity for a younger brother."

"If you make the news, it'll be the notice that you're in the hospital because a big calf threw you."

"You're just jealous because you aren't making a name for yourself like I am." He paused and turned to Dr. Bradley. "Dad," he said with all the seriousness he could muster, "do you think it would be all right with Mr. Calero if I got two or three carloads of guys in my class to come out and watch me ride?"

* * *

Dr. Bradley took Trena out to the Bar T shortly after eight o'clock on Saturday morning. She saddled her horse, made a few practice runs over the barrel race course and stopped, waiting until afternoon before again riding the mare she would be using in the race. She and Bev had made arrangements to go for a ride along the river that

65

morning. They hadn't planned to take Kathy along, but she showed up while they were saddling their horses and wanted to know where they were going. Bev immediately invited her to go along.

They left the ranch buildings and rode across the west pasture toward the river. It was a beautiful, cloudless day. The sun was warm and friendly, coaxing the spring flowers to bloom and the tiny new leaves on the trees to grow. The birds were already back from the south, nesting along the cool river, and their happy voices filled the air.

"This is my favorite time of year," Trena said, standing in the stirrups and looking about. And why wouldn't it be? It was warm and peaceful, she was with her best friend, and they were riding horseback.

"Mine too," Bev added.

Kathy didn't agree with them, however.

"I like summer the best," she said. "School's out then, and we can do all sorts of things, like going on picnics and trail rides and picking wild plums and grapes." She turned to Bev. "And this is going to be the best summer we've ever had. You don't know how nice a summer can be until you've spent one here on the Bar T."

"It does sound nice," Bev answered.

Trena cringed inwardly. Kathy had not included her, that was easy to see. She was thinking only of the times when she and Bev would be alone together. Trena hadn't considered the fact that summer was almost upon them. School would soon be out, and she wouldn't be seeing Bev every day. She would get to see her for only a little while at church on Sundays and occasionally during the week when she invited her over or there was a

66

youth meeting or a party. Kathy and Bev would be together constantly. In spite of herself, jealousy began to creep into Trena's heart again.

Still talking about what she and Bev would do during the summer, Kathy led them through a narrow ravine overgrown with dry sunflower stalks and cockleburs. Trena wasn't aware of the burs until a couple of the prickly balls caught in her horse's mane.

"We're in the burs," she informed her companions.

"They won't hurt anything," Kathy replied. "We're wearing jeans, and the burs won't stick in them."

"But our horses aren't wearing jeans," she countered.

As soon as they were on higher ground once more, Trena dismounted and began to remove the cockleburs from her horse's tail and fetlocks. Kathy was disgusted and wanted to leave her, but Bev also dismounted and began to examine her horse for burs.

"We'll never get anywhere," Kathy grumbled, "if we have to stop and fool around like this all the time."

Trena thought of a number of things she could have said, but decided to keep quiet. Kathy waited impatiently for several minutes while her companions worked at removing the cockleburs. Finally, she could stand it no longer.

"Those things don't hurt a horse any," she said. "He hardly knows that he's picked up a cocklebur, unless he gets one under the saddle. Come on. I've got to work out again before the barrel racing this afternoon, and you ought to work out, too, if you want to get good at it."

But Trena was not going to leave until she had removed the last of the burs. "It'll only take a couple of minutes more."

That did it. Kathy's anger flashed, and she whirled her horse quickly. "You can hang around out here all day for all I care!" she exploded. "I'll be at the ranch."

When she was gone, Bev looked at Trena. "I wish she wasn't like that," she said quietly. "She gets mad over nothing."

"I think she's jealous of you and me being together," Trena said.

"She shouldn't be. The three of us have had some great times. There isn't any reason for her to feel left out."

Trena was thinking about what her dad had said about making friends with Kathy in order to reach her for Christ. It was so easy to talk about doing that. It sounded wonderful at devotions or in a Sunday school class. Everyone agreed that it was what a Christian should do. But putting it into practice with a person like Kathy wasn't quite so simple. She never thought of anyone but herself.

*   *   *

The first event on the rodeo schedule that afternoon was the boys' calf riding. Kathy Downing's younger brother was the first out of the chute. He drew a tough, wiry little animal that gave him plenty of trouble, but he stayed on for the required eight seconds. The next rider wasn't so fortunate. The calf jumped only three times before

68

he sprawled headlong into the dust. Jon, who was sitting on the corral fence, waiting for his name to be called, turned to Tim.

"That guy's got a lot to learn about calf riding," he said confidently.

"Maybe you ought to give him some lessons," Tim said in disgust.

Jon's grin widened. "You know, I was just thinking the same thing myself. I'll bet he'd appreciate having a few hints from an expert."

"Oh, brother! You don't have a very high opinion of yourself, do you?"

"I just face facts, that's all. When a guy's good at something, he ought to admit it. That's what I think."

Before Tim could reply, Jon's name was called.

"I wish you'd brought your camera along," he murmured to Tim as he left his place.

Jon drew a calf that was about the same size as the one he had ridden at the first amateur rodeo. He stopped momentarily just outside the chute and surveyed the calf he would be riding. He had done a lot of brave talking around Tim, but that didn't mean anything now. He still felt uneasy inside. His mouth was dry, and he suddenly felt weak.

"Are you ready, Son?" Mr. Downing asked him.

Jon nodded. "As—as ready as I'll ever be."

He straddled the powerful, iron-muscled calf, tightened his grip on the rope, and nodded to Mr. Downing. The gate swung wide, and the calf exploded into the arena with a savage, stiff-legged jump that jarred Jon's spine and loosened his grip on the rope. With the next jump Jon was spilled into the dust!

Chapter 9

"You Can't Have Her!"

The crowd was laughing as Jon got to his feet and dusted off his jeans. At first he was irritated by their reaction, and his temper flared. Then he recognized a warmth and friendliness in their laughter. They weren't making fun of him, he realized. They were laughing at what had happened and were expecting him to laugh with them. He sauntered slowly out of the big corral, pretending to limp like some of the other riders when they were thrown. He didn't hurt any place, but it seemed that the crowd expected a rider to limp away. He wanted them all to know that he was exactly like the others.

Tim was waiting for him.

"So it finally happened!" he exclaimed triumphantly. "The renowned Mr. Casey Tibbs, the world's greatest rider, got himself bucked off a calf no bigger than his billy goat."

"That was the worst calf anyone here ever tried to ride. And that's a fact." Jon climbed back onto the fence to watch the rest of the go round. He had already decided something—getting thrown by the calf wasn't half as bad as thinking about it had

71

been. He had worried a lot about getting thrown, even when he was talking so big about what a good rider he was. But now that it had happened, he saw that it hadn't even hurt very much.

"You know what, Tim?" he said suddenly.

"I know that calf sure got rid of you in a big hurry," his brother answered.

Jon ignored what Tim said, which surprised his older brother.

"Getting bucked off wasn't so bad. I think I'll try calf riding again at the next rodeo. Maybe I can hang in there the next time."

Tim studied his brother thoughtfully. He had been upset at Jon when he was bragging about how good he was at calf riding and how he was going out on the rodeo circuit as soon as he was old enough. But right now he had to admit that he admired his brother. He took getting thrown the way a man would, without even making any excuses. Maybe Jon was going to amount to something after all, he decided.

The girls' barrel race was the final event of the afternoon. Kathy had saddled her mount before the rodeo began, but Trena waited until a few minutes before the race to saddle her horse. Then she rode him at a slow walk to warm him up. Once she felt that the horse was ready, she rode him at a fast gallop and practiced a few turns.

Bev was the first to be timed in the race. She came across the starting line clumsily, slowed her horse and turned wide around the first barrel with more caution than she had even shown in a practice run. It was plain to everyone in the crowd—even to the Bradleys who were comparatively unfamiliar with the event and its tech-

72

niques—that Bev was not going to do very well. When she crossed the finish line, the crowd clapped their encouragement to her.

"I'm sorry, Mr. Calero," she said apologetically as she dismounted, "but I just couldn't do any better. All I could think of was those barrels and the fact that I had to be careful or I was going to knock one over and disqualify myself."

He held her horse by the reins and patted his nose.

"It really doesn't matter to me whether you win or even place today," he told her. "All I'm concerned about is that you do the very best you can. No one can do any better than that."

She smiled gratefully.

Trena was next. She turned in better time than Bev did, but she was also bothered with the jitters of being in her first race. She almost knocked over a barrel in the first go round, and she disqualified herself by knocking down the third barrel in her final heat.

Kathy, who had been sympathetic and understanding when Bev did so poorly a few minutes before, was aloof and arrogant with Trena.

"You shouldn't feel badly," she said. "Mr. Calero should have known that you weren't ready to race in competition with experienced riders. I blame him for what happened to you this afternoon."

Trena's cheeks flushed, and she fought to control the sudden surge of anger she felt within her. Until now, winning or losing hadn't meant too much to her. She was learning to barrel race simply because she enjoyed it, and winning was secondary.

"Like Mr. Calero told Bev when she apologized

about the way she rode," Trena replied, "the important thing is to do the best you can. I did that, so I don't have anything to apologize for."

"That's probably true," Kathy replied. "But after all, you can't expect to match the time of someone like myself or some of the other girls. You had never heard of barrel racing until this spring."

She probably would have said more, but the announcer called her name, and she mounted her horse for her final go round. Trena found herself wishing that Kathy would knock down a barrel and disqualify herself on her last ride. It would serve her right.

But nothing like that happened. Kathy turned in her best time of the afternoon and beat the other girls by a comfortable margin. The announcer emphasized the fact that her time was close to the record for the county fair.

She came riding back to where Bev and Trena were standing, disdain sharpening the gleam in her eyes. She said nothing; she didn't have to. Her ride, the announcer's words of praise and her own actions spoke louder than anything she could possibly have said. Trena cringed as Kathy dismounted and deliberately turned her back to her in order to talk to Bev.

Kathy's final go round ended the activities for the afternoon, and the visitors began to drift toward their cars, talking as they went. Trena and Bev were leading their horses to the barn to unsaddle and rub them down when Mr. Calero caught up with them.

"I was watching you today, Trena," he said. "I

don't believe it was your fault that you knocked down that barrel."

She faced him silently. That was exactly what Kathy had said. She wondered if he was also going to agree that she wasn't ready for barrel racing. After all, she hadn't done very well. Perhaps he had decided that she was not able to ride as well as he had thought she could.

"The horse you were riding hasn't been used as much as some of the others for barrel racing. I didn't know that when we picked her for you, or we'd have looked at some of the others. I told my wife this morning that I was going to give you a different horse to use in the next race." He glanced over his shoulder in the direction of the Bradley station wagon. "Think your folks have time to wait until we pick out one?"

She was sure they did. They usually spent Saturday afternoon doing something together as a family. They wouldn't mind waiting for a few minutes.

They went behind the barn to the horse corral.

"I've got half a dozen good barrel-racing horses here," he said. "Take your pick."

She looked them over numbly. She hadn't expected anything like this. "Do you really mean it?" she asked.

"If I didn't," he replied, "I wouldn't have said so."

She liked the looks of all of them, but a dark sorrel mare looked far better to her than the rest. She didn't know why, but something about that particular horse appealed to her.

"I think I'll take that one," she said, pointing to the sorrel.

Neither of them knew Kathy was anywhere around until she spoke. "But you can't have her!" she exclaimed suddenly.

Mr. Calero's eyes flashed. He wasn't used to being contradicted. "And why not?"

Kathy's cheeks colored as she realized that she had spoken out in front of the owner of the Bar T Ranch. "I—I'm sorry, Mr. Calero," she stammered. "I—I shouldn't have said anything."

But he was not to be put aside so easily. "What did you mean, Kathy?" he persisted.

She hesitated.

"I—I shouldn't have said anything, especially to you," she repeated. "Just forget it."

He pulled himself erect.

"Kathy, I want to know what you were talking about," he said sternly. "Why did you say that I can't give that horse to Trena to ride?"

"Because Daddy told me that I could use her from now on. I asked him about it after the race today. I was just waiting to start practicing with her, but that's all right. I can pick one of the other horses. It's like Dad says: It's the rider that counts. A good barrel racer can win on most any kind of horse."

But Mr. Calero was not going to brush aside the word of his foreman so easily. It was important for a man to keep his word, he believed.

"No," he said, "your dad is my foreman and is in charge here. If he told you that you could have the mare for barrel racing, that's the way it will be."

A strange look came into her eyes.

"You don't have to check with him," Kathy said quickly. "Just let Trena have the sorrel." By

76

this time she was close to tears. "I can beat her anyway. I don't care what horse she's riding!"

Trena wondered if Mr. Calero had seen the dismay in Kathy's eyes when she thought he was going to talk to her father. But if he noticed, he said nothing about it.

"No, I'm not going to check with him, Kathy," he answered. "You've told me what he said; that's good enough for me."

Her relief was evident.

"Pick out another horse, Trena," the rancher said. "Lady is top notch, but there are two or three others that are just as good as she is. Take Pancho, the bay in the corner. He would be my pick."

She studied the horses carefully. None appealed to her as much as Lady, but she had to choose one. If she didn't, Mr. Calero would be unhappy. She said that she would take the horse he suggested. It would be as good as any.

"Fine!" Mr. Calero exclaimed. "You'll like Pancho. He'll put you right out front if you give him half a chance."

Kathy's smile was almost a smirk.

Chapter 10

Called Into the Office

Trena was sure Kathy Downing had lied to Mr. Calero when she told him that her dad said she could use the sorrel mare in the barrel races. Something about the way she looked caused Trena to believe she had said that only to keep Trena from getting the horse she really wanted. But Trena said nothing to anyone about her suspicion. She didn't even mention it to Bev. She was afraid that her friend would believe she was talking about Kathy because she didn't like her. And Trena didn't want that.

Besides, the horse she rode in the barrel race didn't make that much difference to her. In fact, she liked the one Mr. Calero suggested to her almost as much as the sorrel mare. She was sure she would be able to do as well riding Pancho as she would have done with Lady. She did not agree with the rancher that her trouble in the race that day was because of the horse she used. The problem was more likely her own inexperience. She just didn't know enough about barrel racing.

She soon discovered, however, that having a well-trained horse did make a great deal of

79

difference. Blaze was spirited and fast, but she could not be compared to Pancho. The sturdy bay knew exactly what he was doing. At the touch of her heels in his flanks he broke across the starting line at top speed, spun tightly around the first barrel and blasted across the arena to the second. He seemed to understand the purpose of the race and was determined to turn in the best time possible. Once Trena became familiar with his speed and his quick turns, she would be able to compete with the best of the girls who entered the ranch rodeos. For that reason she continued to go out to the Bar T to ride two or three times a week.

It seemed to her that Kathy tried to avoid her in the days that followed, as though she was ashamed of something she had done. She did a lot of practicing with Lady, and she was often using the barrel race course when Trena came out to practice. When that happened, Kathy would leave abruptly. Even Bev noticed and remarked about it, wondering why she always left when Trena came around.

"She's never said anything to me about why she doesn't stay," Trena said. "Has she mentioned it to you?"

Bev frowned and shook her head. "The only thing she's said to me is that she thinks you don't like her."

Trena did not reply. What could she say? Kathy was close to the truth. Trena didn't think she really disliked her, but the other girl didn't do much to make her want to be around her.

"If we could just reach her for Christ," Bev said seriously, "a lot of these things would change."

Trena nodded. That was Kathy's biggest problem, she decided, agreeing with her friend. Kathy simply did not know the Lord.

"I had a chance to share Christ with her last night," she went on, keeping her voice low. "We had a long talk—for an hour or more. She acts as though she wants to become a Christian, but something is holding her back. I can't understand it."

Again, Bev asked Trena to pray for her as she talked with their new friend, and she promised that she would. Trena relayed the request to the rest of the family. She also asked them to pray for her performance in the barrel race the following Saturday. Everyone seemed to expect her to do so well, and she felt that she knew absolutely nothing about riding, especially in comparison to the other girls.

Tim glanced at Jon and then back at his sister.

"Why don't you get Casey Tibbs the second to teach you?" he asked. "Of course, he specializes in calf riding, but I've got a hunch that he wouldn't let a little thing like that bother him. You could be persuaded to give her a few pointers, couldn't you, Mr. Tibbs?"

Jon's cheeks crimsoned. "Lay off, will you?"

But Tim wasn't about to stop. "A real expert like you ought to be willing to share what he knows with his sister," he continued. "You'd expect her to help you if she knew all about it and you were just learning, wouldn't you?"

"I'd expect somebody to keep his mouth shut," Jon muttered.

"You shouldn't tease Jon that way, Tim," Mrs. Bradley said.

"That's right," Dr. Bradley said. "I believe we've had quite enough talk about the subject."

Jon looked up at them gratefully. His folks really knew when a guy needed help. It wasn't that he blamed Tim all that much for teasing him. He had to admit that he had asked for it. He was beginning to wish that he had never seen a calf.

Next Saturday, he promised himself, he would stay on his calf if it killed him. He had to prove to Tim and his dad and everyone else that he could ride. He didn't know why he felt that way, but staying on a calf for eight seconds meant a great deal to him right then.

*   *   *

Jon had a good opportunity to get out of the calf riding at the next Bar T rodeo. Something came up at the last minute that kept his folks from attending. No one would have thought anything about it if he hadn't come either. But he couldn't do that. He had to get out there and prove himself, if he could. He asked for a ride with Mr. Grantham when he stopped by for Trena.

None of the calves used in the boys' calf riding were particularly wild or mean, but a few were more lively and unpredictable than the rest. And Jon drew one of those calves. The young animal was big and rawboned, with eyes that rolled as the boy settled on his back and grabbed the rope with his right hand. Breathing a prayer for God's strength and help, he nodded to the man at the gate.

It swung open, and the calf exploded from the chute, stiff legged and whirling. Jon clung

82

desperately to the rope, his heels clamped against the calf's sides. It wasn't a beautiful ride. He first slipped to one side and then to the other. One instant he felt as though he was about to slide over the calf's head. The next he was about to pitch backward into the dust. But somehow he stayed on.

The whistle sounded at the end of eight seconds, but that didn't mean a thing to the youthful rider. He was in a personal battle with that calf, and it wasn't over yet. He hung on frantically while the calf bucked and pitched just as violently as he had the moment he was turned loose. Finally, Jon could stay aboard no longer. His fingers slipped a little with each wild jump until the rope pulled out of his grasp. The next jump loosened his legs and sent him flying. A roar of applause went up from the crowd. He had given a good ride—the best of the day—and they were recognizing him for it.

Jon got up slowly, ignoring the sharp pain in his hip, and dusted himself off. He had done it again. He didn't blame Tim for getting on his back after all his bragging about how good he was. He certainly had made a fool of himself and the rest of the family. He only wished that his older brother hadn't come out to the rodeo that afternoon. Jon supposed Tim would be happy now that he'd seen him get clobbered again.

He was just coming through the fence when Tim hurried over to him.

"Hey, man!" he exclaimed. "That was great!"

The younger boy scowled. "You don't have to rub it in."

"No foolin'! That was a great ride! I was proud of you!"

83

"Knock it off, will you? You know I got thrown."

"Sure, you got thrown," Tim admitted, "but not until after you stayed on him twice as long as anyone else has done today. If they were giving prize money today, you'd have won first prize by a mile."

Jon still thought his older brother was kidding. Any minute he would start laughing about the way he got thrown. But he didn't. He acted as though he really meant it. For a while Jon could not understand what was going on. He wouldn't believe Tim until several others, including Mr. Calero, told him how well he had done. Jon thanked God for helping him. He couldn't understand it, but he felt much different now than he had after successfully riding his first calf. This time he was thankful for being able to prove to himself that he could do it, but he didn't have the pride and arrogance he had before. Actually, he didn't even feel like talking to anyone about it.

Trena also did better in the barrel race than she ever had before, but Kathy was still ahead of her by a narrow margin. Trena had just finished her third and final go round when Mr. Calero told her that he wanted to talk to her in his office as soon as she finished taking care of her horse. His lips were tight, and his steel-gray eyes were hard and cold. She wondered what she had done to cause him to stare at her like that.

Bev and Kathy were both ordered to the rancher's office as well. They were talking about it as they took care of their horses in the barn when the rodeo was over.

84

"What do you suppose he wants?" Bev asked curiously.

Kathy glared at Trena.

"What did you tell him?"

Trena didn't know what she was talking about and told her so.

"You ought to know," Kathy retorted. "What did you tell him about me?"

"I haven't even talked with Mr. Calero about you. Actually, your name hasn't come up since the day he gave me Pancho to ride."

Kathy was furious.

"Don't try to tell me that! I know better!"

Chapter 11

"You Lied to Me!"

The fact that Mr. Calero wanted to talk to them was disturbing to the girls. He had always approached them casually wherever they were, but this time he insisted that they meet him in his office. There had to be an important reason for it.

They finished taking care of their horses as quickly as possible and went to Mr. Calero's home, where they knocked timidly on the door. His wife let them in and took them to his office. On previous occasions when Trena had seen her, she had been warm and friendly. Now, however, she acted as though she scarcely knew them. She certainly didn't act as though she liked them.

"You can wait here," she said coolly. "Gerard will be here in a few moments." With that, she closed the door and left them alone in the large office.

Kathy squirmed nervously.

"Why do you suppose he wants to talk to us?" she asked of no one in particular.

Neither Trena nor Bev had any idea.

"I still say you must have told him something, Trena," she said accusingly.

She denied it, but it didn't do any good. Kathy did not believe her and said so.

"What could I have told Mr. Calero that would have made him mad at all of us?" Trena asked seriously. She had no idea what could have caused the ranch owner to want to see the three of them. All she knew was that it must be something important, and from the way Mrs. Calero acted, it must be something he didn't like.

Before Kathy spoke again, the door opened and Mr. Calero came in. The lanky rancher spoke curtly to them and went around behind his desk to sit down. He looked at them for a moment, studying each frightened young face, before he leaned forward to rest his elbows on the desk.

"I suppose you are wondering what this is all about," he began after a time.

They nodded hesitantly.

"At first I was going to talk to you alone, Kathy," he said. "After all, you are the one who is primarily involved. Then I decided it would be best to have Bev and Trena here too."

Dismay flecked Kathy's eyes.

"W-w-what do you want to talk to me about?" she asked meekly.

His gaze met hers and held it.

"Don't you know?"

Her cheeks reddened. "S-should I?"

Mr. Calero's eyes blazed. "Yes, Kathy, you should know why I've called you in. You lied to me, and I don't like it. If there is anything that makes me angry, it is to have someone lie to me."

She moistened her lips with the tip of her tongue. She acted as though she wanted to speak but remained silent.

88

He turned to Trena. "You know what I'm talking about, don't you?" He continued without waiting for her to answer. "I saw it in your eyes that day at the corral. You knew that Kathy was lying. Isn't that right?"

There was a long silence. She nodded almost imperceptibly. There was no need for her to say anything. She knew Mr. Calero was talking about the sorrel mare she had picked out and Kathy's insistence that her dad had already told her she could have Lady for the barrel races.

"Kathy," the rancher said, his voice as hushed as the wind just before a storm, "why did you tell me something that wasn't true?"

"I—I . . ." Her voice trailed off miserably. She acted as though she had something she wanted to say but could not force out the words.

"Have I ever been unfair to you?" he wanted to know. "Have I ever denied you a good horse to ride in the barrel races?"

She shook her head.

"Didn't you know that there are a dozen horses on the ranch that are as well trained and as fast as Lady?"

He waited for almost a minute for her to speak, and only when he saw that she was going to remain silent did he continue.

"When you told me your dad said you could have Lady for barrel racing, I wondered about it, but I took your word for it. Then later I found out the truth. Like I said, if there is anything I detest, it is having someone lie to me. I've fired men who have worked on this ranch for 20 years because they lied to me. I have always said that if someone lies to me once and I find out about it, it's his

89

fault. If he lies to me the second time, it's my fault. Do you understand what I mean?"

His words seemed to loosen Kathy's tongue. She took a deep breath and began to explain frantically. "I really didn't lie to you, Mr. Calero. I talked to Daddy a long time ago about riding Lady in the barrel races. You may not believe me, and I suppose he must have forgotten about it, but I'm telling you the truth. I—"

The ranch owner did not allow her to continue.

"Kathy!" he reproved her sternly. "Don't make things any worse for yourself than they are already. The truth is that you didn't even think about riding Lady until Trena picked her out. You picked out the horse you're riding now and told me at the time that he was your favorite. But when Trena said she liked Lady, you came up with that story about your dad giving her to you for the races. You did it to keep Trena from having her. Isn't that right?"

She had no answer.

"You've been almost like a daughter to me, Kathy. There are few things on this ranch I would have denied you if you had come to me and asked for them. But I can't have you or anyone else lying to me. You know that I can't let you keep Lady after what has happened, don't you?"

"But I—" she began in desperation.

"I'm not even sure I'm going to allow you to compete in the Bar T rodeos for the rest of this season. I'll have to think on it and talk with your dad about it to see what he wants me to do."

The rancher directed his attention to Trena, offering to let her ride Lady in the rest of the races that summer. The offer was tempting because she

90

still believed the sorrel was the prettiest horse she had ever seen. But she decided that she was doing well on Pancho and didn't want to change. Besides, she didn't want to use the horse that had been Kathy's. Even if she was a better horse—which she doubted—she didn't want to benefit by what had happened to Kathy.

"You can think about it if you want to," he told her when she said she wanted to keep the horse she was riding, "and let me know what you've decided the next time you come out to see the girls."

As far as he was concerned, that ended the discussion. He got to his feet and came back around the desk. Kathy's lips were quivering when the girls left the rancher's house, but she managed not to cry.

"We're sorry," Bev told her simply.

She stopped at the gate, belligerence glazing her eyes and tightening her thin lips.

"I'll bet you are!" she glared at Trena. "This was all your fault! You told Mr. Calero that I lied to him. You're the one who turned him against me."

"I didn't say anything to him or to anyone else," Trena said. "How could I have known that you weren't telling the truth? I didn't know you hadn't asked your dad for Lady."

"A fine friend you turned out to be!" Kathy exploded, as though everything that had happened was Trena's fault. "And you try to talk to me about becoming a Christian! If a Christian acts like you do, I don't want to be one. That's for sure!"

Trena pulled in a deep breath. She didn't know why Kathy had to talk that way to her. She

91

honestly hadn't said anything to Mr. Calero, to Bev or even to her mother about what she suspected.

She did have to admit that she wasn't as sorry for Kathy as she could have been. Actually, she wasn't sorry for her at all. The way she looked at it, Kathy got what she deserved. Like Mr. Calero said, she hadn't even wanted Lady for herself. At least she hadn't wanted her badly enough to talk with her dad about getting the beautiful sorrel to ride in the barrel races. Kathy had known that Trena wanted Lady and was determined to keep her from getting the little mare. That was the reason she had said what she did.

Trena didn't know why Kathy would turn against her so bitterly unless she was jealous of her friendship with Bev or was afraid that Trena might beat her in the races if she got a better horse.

Trena Bradley knew that her dad would feel the same as Mr. Calero about lying. He always said that lying was one thing he would punish his children for quicker than for anything else. He said that a person who would lie couldn't be trusted at all—for anything.

She was glad now that she hadn't said anything to Bev about Kathy and the horse she wanted to use for racing. If she had, her friend might suspect that she had gone to the rancher in an effort to get Kathy in trouble. Now she could tell Bev honestly that she had nothing to do with it.

When Kathy was gone, Bev turned back to Trena.

"I don't know why Kathy says things like that about you," she said sorrowfully. "She doesn't really mean them."

The two girls crossed the yard together. Trena

didn't say anything. There was nothing she could say. She couldn't understand why Bev was always sticking up for Kathy. No matter what happened, she tried to find something good to say about her. There were times when it seemed to Trena that Bev actually took Kathy's side against her.

"Kathy is going to feel just terrible if she doesn't get to ride in the barrel races for the rest of the summer," Bev said. "Do you suppose it would do any good if you and I would go to Mr. Calero and ask if he would let her enter the races?"

Trena eyed her friend questioningly. She didn't know whether she wanted Kathy to ride in the rest of the races or not. She certainly didn't deserve to after what she had done.

"What do you think?" Bev asked her again.

Trena hesitated.

"I don't know," she answered, hoping her friend wouldn't suspect how she really felt. "Mr. Calero doesn't seem to me to be the kind who would change his mind."

"But you will go with me to see him, won't you?"

Chapter 12

Kathy's Punishment

Trena was surprised to see that Bev was about to cry.

"The least we can do is talk to Mr. Calero," the Grantham girl continued. "I thought maybe he would listen to you more than he would to me."

Trena could scarcely believe that Bev would even expect her to plead with the rancher for Kathy.

"I wouldn't go to see him alone," she said, hedging. "I couldn't do that."

"You wouldn't have to go alone. I'd be with you. You're the one who was actually hurt by what Kathy did. I figured maybe he would consider that and be more likely to do what you asked than he would if I wanted him to let her ride in the barrel races again."

Trena scuffed the dirt with the pointed toe of her cowboy boot. She didn't understand why Bev thought she would have more influence over Mr. Calero than she would. Even if she did have some influence, she didn't know whether or not she wanted to use it for Kathy's sake. Kathy deserved to be punished for what she had done. That was the only way she would learn not to do it again.

Still, Trena found it hard to refuse her friend. "Why don't we pray about it for a couple of days before we do anything?" she asked. "Then we'll be sure that we're doing the right thing."

Reluctantly, Bev agreed. She would have preferred talking with the rancher right away, but she supposed that waiting and praying was best. It was always best to pray first. That way they would have the assurance that God was guiding them.

"I'm going to talk to Kathy now," Bev said. "Maybe this trouble with Mr. Calero will help her see that she needs Christ as her Saviour."

Trena doubted that there would be any dramatic change in the other girl because of what had happened, but she didn't say that to Bev. Her friend felt too unhappy already.

"Pray for me," she murmured.

Trena walked to the Grantham pickup to wait for her friend's father. She thought Bev would be coming along when he drove her home. She always had on other occasions, but this time she stayed with Kathy. Trena found that very disturbing. Bev was almost acting as if Kathy was the one who had been wronged. It made Trena feel as though she was in second place as far as Bev's affections were concerned.

*   *   *

That night during their evening devotions, Dr. Bradley asked for prayer requests. Trena intended to say that she had an unspoken request so she wouldn't have to make an explanation. But she found herself relating the entire story. When she had finished, Dr. Bradley looked from one member of the family to another.

"Tell me, Jon," he said, "what do you think Trena ought to do?"

"She ought to forget about that Kathy," he retorted. "She's been bad news ever since Bev moved out to the ranch."

"Maybe she's learned her lesson," Cindy said tenderly. "Maybe if Trena goes to Mr. Calero with Bev and gets him to let Kathy race again, she'll be so happy about it she'll become a Christian."

They discussed the matter for several minutes before Dr. Bradley asked Tim to lead them in prayer. Trena was disappointed. She had expected her parents to give her more guidance.

"But, Dad," she exclaimed. "What do you think I should do?"

He studied her pretty young face thoughtfully.

"I think we should ask the Lord to guide you, Trena," he said.

"But—"

"Of course, there are some questions you will have to answer for yourself. Why is it that you are uncertain about what you should do? Is it because you don't want Kathy in the races against you? Is it because you want to see her punished for what she did to you? Or is it because you honestly believe she needs to be punished in order to learn a lesson about lying? Our motives are always most important."

Trena hesitated. At first she was sure that her motives were pure and that all the fault was Kathy's. She didn't think she had anything against her. How could she have anything against Kathy? She had been praying that she would put her trust in Jesus Christ. But did she really love Kathy and want to see her become a Christian? Honestly? Did she have even half the love for the other girl that Bev had?

It was easy for her to say that she did, but did she actually love Kathy? Before God, could she say that she did? Her mind raced, and she had little peace, even after they had prayed. How could she know what she should do when she couldn't even answer the questions her dad asked?

Long after the rest of the house was dark and quiet, Trena was still wide awake, staring up at the ceiling. She had finally decided to go with Bev to see Mr. Calero about Kathy. She thought that once she told the Lord about her decision, she would have peace. It did not come, however. She was still deeply troubled.

* * *

When school was out Monday afternoon, Trena went out to the Bar T. She and Bev went to Mr. Calero's office to talk to him about their friend. He couldn't understand why they had decided to come and see him and wanted to know if Kathy had asked them to do so.

"No," Bev replied quietly. "Kathy doesn't even know we're here. We didn't say anything to her about it, and she hasn't said anything to us."

"I must confess that you girls have amazed me by this visit," he said at last. "I would like to do what you ask because it is so unselfish. Still, we've got to think about Kathy and what's best for her. If we let her off easily this time, she may find it too easy to lie the next time she feels like it." He drew himself erect. "I don't like to have to tell you this, but I'm afraid I'm going to have to stick with what I told her."

Nevertheless, he followed them to the door, talking to them warmly. When they were on the porch of the Calero home, Trena saw that Kathy was standing in the doorway of the barn watching them. As she looked up, Kathy stepped back into the darkness of the barn's interior.

* * *

The Bar T was having another rodeo Saturday afternoon, and Trena went out again to ride in the barrel race. She saddled Pancho and warmed him up carefully. For some reason, she didn't have the enthusiasm for the barrel race that day that she had felt on previous occasions. Not having Kathy in the race almost ruined it for her.

"You know, Bev," she said. "I really wish that Kathy was racing today. It's not going to be nearly as much fun without her."

"I feel the same way." Bev looked up, her eyes searching the crowd for their friend. "I feel so sorry for her, I can hardly stand it."

"Maybe if we talked to Mr. Calero again, he would let her in the race," Trena suggested.

Bev didn't think it would do any good after the way he had talked to them earlier in the week, but she figured it wouldn't hurt to try. He just might change his mind about Kathy.

They found him at the chutes and called him to one side to ask again if Kathy could be in the race.

"You two won't take no for an answer, will you?" he asked.

Trena didn't know what she said in reply, but Mr. Calero's expression changed.

"Do you really mean that you honestly want her in the race? Riding Lady?"

That was exactly what she wanted, she told him. When she and Bev had talked to him earlier in the week, she really hadn't cared all that much, but now she was anxious to have Kathy in the race.

He frowned thoughtfully. "I'll tell you what I'll do," he said. "Let her stay out of the race today. She hasn't been working out all week, so she wouldn't do very well anyway. When the rodeo is over today, I'll hunt her up and tell her that she'll be able to race from now on. How's that?"

They both thanked him, grateful for the change in his attitude.

Bev wanted to tell Kathy what Mr. Calero had said, but she decided against it. It would be better if the information came from the rancher.

Trena was walking around with Pancho when she heard a couple of the other girls talking.

"It's too bad about Kathy's hard luck, isn't it?" one of them said. "It's tough having your horse go lame just before a race. If it had happened a couple of days ago, she could have worked out with another one and done all right, but as it is, she had to drop out."

The other girl shook her head. "I know how terrible I'd feel if that happened to me. You'd think she would risk using another horse in a case like this, wouldn't you? There's surely another good horse on a ranch as large as this one that Mr. Calero would let her ride."

100

"What good would it do?" her friend countered. "I'm sure I'd knock down every barrel if I had to change horses without working out two or three times. I don't care how good the replacement horse was."

Trena tied Pancho to the corral fence and went to get a drink of water. So that was the story Kathy was telling to keep everyone from knowing the real reason she wasn't in the barrel race. Mr. Calero had been right. Kathy had a lesson to learn about lying. But she hadn't learned it yet. And now Trena and Bev had talked him into letting her race again. She felt sick inside.

The first rider in the girls' barrel race turned in excellent time—at least two seconds better than Trena's best time. It looked as though it was going to be a tough race all the way. The announcer called out her name, and she loosened Pancho's reins and put one foot in the stirrup.

The instant the horse felt her weight on the saddle he began to fidget strangely. He had never done that before, but she paid little attention to it as she swung her weight into the saddle.

Then Pancho exploded! He reared first, so high she was sure he was going to fall backward with her. Then he jerked his head down between his legs and began to buck!

Chapter 13

Trena's Bucking Horse

Trena fought hard to stay on the wildly bucking horse. Clinging to Pancho's sweating shoulders with her knees, she yanked on the reins in a vain attempt to pull his head up, taking the violence out of his bucking. But he was much too powerful for her. He lunged forward, frantically trying to free himself of the terrible weight on his back.

At first, the crowd clapped and yelled with delight at Trena and Pancho. After two or three jumps, however, they realized that something was wrong, and an awed hush fell over everyone. Trena began to ride a bit more confidently as she stayed on him through the first spine-jarring jumps. Some of the fire was going out of the suddenly crazed animal, and she thought she was going to be able to bring him under control.

Then Pancho seemed to explode with a new burst of energy. His head came up a little, and she yanked savagely on the reins. Then without warning, he threw his head back and reared, teetering as he fought Trena violently. Then he lost his balance and toppled backward.

103

An instant before it happened, she realized he was going to fall and wrenched one foot free of the stirrup. Another fraction of a second and she would have been free, but it didn't work out that way. The full weight of the horse crashed on her leg! Excruciating pain shot up into her thigh, consuming her entire being. Mercifully, she blacked out.

Trena didn't know who rushed over and examined her first or who called the Emergency Unit from town. She remembered stirring once or twice and opening her eyes to see her mother bending over her. Then she drifted into unconsciousness again. It was the middle of the following day when she regained consciousness for good. She opened her eyes and saw her parents sitting by her bed.

"How do you feel, Trena?" Dr. Bradley asked quietly.

She grimaced. "Lousy!"

"Did you know that your right leg is broken?"

She reached down and felt the cast on her leg. She couldn't seem to remember what had happened, but the news that her leg was broken came as no surprise to her.

"The doctor X-rayed it and set it this morning."

She nodded. Now that he mentioned it, she remembered talking briefly to him and being wheeled down to the X-ray room at the end of the hall and later to the operating room, where her leg was set and the cast was put on. She lay silently for a long while, waiting until the nurse came in and took her temperature and gave her another injection. When she and her parents were alone in the room again, she asked what had happened.

Her dad told her as much as he knew about the accident, relating how Pancho had started to buck unexpectedly and then had fallen over backward, catching her leg between the ground and the saddle. It had been a close call, he said. She could have been caught directly under the horse. God had been gracious in helping her to avoid a more serious injury, or even death.

She thought about what had happened. She couldn't figure out why the horse had bucked like that. One of the reasons she liked riding Pancho so much was his disposition and reliability. It wasn't like him to suddenly go mad and buck like a rodeo bronc.

"Why would Pancho do a thing like that anyway, Dad?" she asked after a time. "He's always been so gentle. He's as easy to handle as any of the other horses on the ranch."

"According to Mr. Calero, he had good reason for it," he said, his face dark with indignation. "Someone put cockleburs under your saddle."

She gasped. "Are you sure?"

"I'm positive," he nodded. "I saw them myself."

"Who would do a thing like that, Jonathan?" Mrs. Bradley wanted to know. "It couldn't have been an accident."

"You're right about that. It couldn't have been an accident." He paused as though uncertain about saying more. "When I talked to Gerard about it, he said that he has a good idea who was responsible for it. He's going to look into the matter right away and get to the bottom of it, if he can."

Mrs. Bradley went over to her daughter's bed and took her hand protectively. "I can't imagine anyone disliking Trena so much they would do a thing like that to her. There must be some mistake."

Trena said nothing. She didn't have to speculate about it. There was only one person who could have done it! She closed her eyes wearily. She didn't even want to think about what had happened. It gave her a sick feeling inside. She decided to talk to Bev about it when she came to the hospital to see her.

But that didn't happen right away. The doctor found that she had a slight concussion, so he had a "No Visitors" sign placed on her door for a few days so she could have complete bed rest. He told her he didn't like to do it, but he knew her friends would be flocking in to see her, and he didn't believe it was good for her to have a lot of company right then. When he finally allowed her to have visitors other than the members of her family, Bev was the first to come and see her.

"I've brought someone with me to see you," Bev told her. "Is it all right if I bring her in?"

Trena couldn't imagine who it would be. She decided it was probably one of the girls from school. Bev went to the door and waited for what seemed like several minutes. Then Kathy Downing appeared in the doorway, her lips quivering with emotion. Mechanically, she stepped into the room, and Bev closed the door behind her.

"H-Hello, Trena," she managed, her voice small and thin.

The girl in the hospital bed spoke to her.

106

"I imagine you're surprised to see me," she continued.

Trena nodded.

Again there was a long, painful silence. Kathy had something to tell Trena, but it wasn't easy. She fought to force out the words.

"I—I don't even know how to begin," she stammered, "but I—I—I've got to tell you about—"

"I know," Trena broke in. "You put cockleburs under my saddle before I rode in the barrel race."

The other girl's eyes widened.

"Did Mr. Calero tell you?"

"This is the first day I've had company other than members of my family," Trena answered. "I haven't even seen Mr. Calero. If you want to know the truth, nobody told me. I knew that you were the one who must have done it."

Kathy tried to speak once more but started to cry. It was several minutes before she could continue.

"I have been so jealous of you I could hardly stand it. You were Bev's best friend, and I—I've lived alone at the ranch as long as I can remember—as far as being around other girls my age is concerned. You had all kinds of friends at school. Bev was the only friend I had a chance of having. And you could ride so well you began to do almost as well as the rest of us in the barrel race. Then when I couldn't ride b-b-because of what I did, I figured that I had to do something to get even. I—I'm sorry."

Trena didn't say anything to her right then. She was thinking about her own attitude toward the other girl. She hadn't realized that Kathy was a

107

lonely person who needed friends. She had been so jealous—so wrapped up in herself—that she wanted Bev for herself. She didn't want any other friends, and she especially didn't want Bev to have any other friends.

"Will you forgive me?" Kathy said.

"Of course I'll forgive you," Trena said, tears filling her own eyes. "But you aren't the only one who's at fault. I've got to ask your forgiveness too. If—if I had treated you the way I should have, probably none of this would have happened."

Kathy stared at her. "You can't mean that! Not after what I did to you!"

"But I do," Trena assured her.

Kathy started to cry again. She was still crying when the nurse came in and told her and Bev that visiting hours were over and that they would have to leave.

"You'll come back again tomorrow, won't you?" Trena asked.

"Do you want me to?" Kathy asked uncertainly.

"You know I do."

*   *   *

As soon as school was out the following day, Bev and Kathy were back at the hospital to see Trena. This time their eyes were shining with excitement.

"Kathy has something she wants to tell you, Trena," Bev began.

Kathy went over to the bed and took Trena's hand. "I'm a Christian now, Trena," she said quietly, "just like you and Bev."

"That's wonderful!"

"When I first started running around with Bev and you, she began talking to me about going to church and Sunday school. She tried to share Christ with me, but I felt that I didn't need a Saviour. This is going to sound terrible, but I figured I didn't have to go to church or to trust Christ. I figured I was just as good as you were.

"When I came in here yesterday to tell you I was sorry, I—I really wasn't—not deep in my heart. I came because my folks made me. But when you asked my forgiveness after the terrible thing I had done to you, I—I couldn't stand it. I saw that you and Bev had something I didn't have."

Again she started to cry and wiped at the tears in her eyes.

"So," she continued, "after we left the hospital, I admitted to God that I was a sinner, and I put my trust in Jesus Christ when Bev talked with me about Him again."

Trena grabbed Kathy by the hand and pulled her down to her, holding her tightly.

"I—I went and talked to Mr. Calero last night," she said. "I—I told him what had happened to me and asked him to forgive me too. It seemed to shake him up. He said he was going to talk to your dad in a day or two. He figured anyone who would do what you have done must have something genuine. He even said that if it would make me come and tell him I was sorry, it was worth looking into."

A smile lighted Trena's thin face. God was good!